ALL THAT IS BEHIND US NOW

ALL THAT IS BEHIND US NOW

TRICIA YOST

Radial Books

Also by Tricia Yost
First Things
Votives: Entries from the Daybooks of Gertrude Tate, 1898-1952
Factory

Published by Radial Books
radialbooks.com

All That is Behind Us Now/ Tricia Yost, 1st ed.

ISBN: 978-0-9984146-5-2

Cover Art: *Touching Me Softly*, Anette Lusher, 2016.

Typesetting services by BOOKOW.COM

"One should not believe too strongly in a life which can easily vanish."

JAMES SALTER, A Sport and a Pastime

Contents

FIDDLEHEAD

A year ago I would mash my head into the pillow, arrange my neck and face for comfort, then drop into a deep sleep within minutes. Now I don't sleep well. I wake sweating, my pelvis and right thigh aching.

"Liz, you're here. Home. You're safe." I know Abby's voice immediately. Her hand cools the sweaty slope of my back. She places her other hand below my left breast. "Your heart."

I focus on my breath, exhaling longer than I inhale. My heart rate slows. "My leg aches," I say.

Abby reaches for the gel and kneads it into the skin and muscle around the scar. Her touch, soft at first, shifts toward insistence.

I kiss her neck, then I hold her wrist, stilling her movement. "Wash your hand." She dutifully washes the gel from her hand. She takes longer than I think necessary. She slides her clean hand between my thighs. Takes my breath. My focus shifts away from the deeper ache. Her touch is one of the few things that soothes me. The ferry horn bellows. Fog. My heart pummels itself as Abby brings me to orgasm. My body is silent, the respite brief. The ache returns.

"I'm going for a walk," I say.

"It's late."

"I know."

"Do you want company?"

"No, go back to sleep."

Abby is used to this, and has stopped protesting. She relaxes her head back on the pillow. "Take the dog," she says.

"We don't have a dog."

"I need to get you a dog." She is soon asleep.

For a time in my life I was ambitious and excitable. I cared about my career. I dragged Abby to concerts, Shakespeare in the Park, holiday musicals, and little-known plays. In Cincinnati, I shoved her into jazz nights at Kaldi's and open readings in coffee houses. In Seattle, I made her go rollerblading on Alki, to development meetings, to block parties. I joined a volleyball league and a shuffleboard club. To be a part of things. Alive in the world. Abby and I went skiing and took trips. We toured English gardens in Canada and walked twelve miles along the rim of the Grand Canyon. For a large part of my life things were expected of me, big and small. Being the middle child, born to a lawyer mother and a PhD father, I was expected to graduate from college, have a career, if not kids, do good things and lead a good life. And I did, for a long time, fulfill expectations.

But then. A girl with a gun. In Nowhere Colorado. Gun girl. Gun boys. Fourteen hospital days. Twelve weeks off my feet. Holes in my belly, fractured bones, ambitions bled white. Nightmares kept away any thoughts of future projects. All I did for several days after returning from the hospital was inch my pelvis around the bed in search of comfort. I could only breathe through fascial pull and pain, breathe through the mind's call not to.

You'll never get through this.

Don't focus on the pain.

Recovery. Recovery.

Look at Abby.

Now I am walking, not normally, not as before, but I am moving. Night walks. Without destination. Skulking steps in the dark across arbitrary neighborhood boundaries. I can walk anywhere, slowly but anywhere. My right leg hasn't regained its muscle mass, nor its former strength and endurance. I walk at night because the night holds silence yet divests itself of secrets. It also conceals my limp.

I don't know who shot me, the girl or one of the two boys. Knowing doesn't matter.

I wake with a start. Gunshots in my dream. Abby's hand on my back.

"Don't go out tonight," she says.

"I have to. I have to do something."

"Do this," she says, taking my hand and putting it between her legs. I do. I slide into her. We kiss and roll and smash our bodies together. She lurches with climax. I lay with her for a few minutes before shifting to sit on the side of the bed.

"Wait," she says. She gets up, pulls the chain to the attic stairs and climbs. I step into the doorway to see the rump of my cello case emerge from the ceiling. Abby carefully lowers the awkward bulk and carefully lowers herself.

"The noise will keep you awake," I say. I pick mindlessly at the most superficial layer of tattoo on my shoulder. Fresh blood pools around the scab.

"I don't sleep well when you're out at night. I'd rather have you here. Tomorrow we can clear out the shed and line it with eggshell pads. I see what you're doing with the walking and

3

the tattoos. You're trying to contain the terror, put a form to it without exposing yourself, but that's an impossible task."

Abby had studied art and artists. She couldn't help over-applying what they taught her. I looked at the fine lines aging her eyes. I felt like I hadn't looked at her in years.

"Ink and February are not your forms," she continued. "They're foreign for you. There are forms that come naturally and that are good for you. But not those."

February. Our name for her days in Ohio and my bruised wrists and twisted nights with Rebecca, though Abby doesn't know yet about Rebecca.

Does it count if I kept my clothes on?

Does it count if I didn't come?

Does it count if it won't happen again?

Does it count if I didn't enjoy it?

Does it count if I'm recovering for having done it?

Rebecca and I knew each other when we were young, hormonal, and impassioned. Long ago. We knew each other when we could be brutal in our actions and honesty. I did things with her that I could never do with Abby. We can't get everything from one person.

"Walking is good for me."

"The cello, on the other hand, goes back to your childhood, so it's almost innate."

"I like walking."

"You come home limping every morning. You're ruined all that day and the next."

"So what?"

"Can we please just buy a treadmill?"

I don't get up. I look toward our latest print on the wall. The neighbors' deck light illuminates *Moment*, another Newman.

Abby picked it up during her time in Cincinnati. *Moment*: vertical with a strong pale yellow zip dividing or joining the panels into equal parts. The center band contrasts the panels of streaked browns, greens, whites, grays. The right most panel resembles a figure screaming. While chronologically possible, Munch's work might inform this painting, but not likely. Newman, as did others, stopped working in response to World War II because no art forms were commensurate to the crisis. Newman even destroyed everything he did before 1944. He had to begin again. He dated *Moment* to 1946, after the war had ended, after his own re-emergence.

I ask, "Do you ever wonder if we're not doing enough with our lives?"

"Not especially. I came to terms with that question years ago."

"And it never needled you again?"

"I don't let it. I'd be an indecisive and ineffectual mess. I'm okay with my quiet life."

"Think about it. There are people out there who save lives. The medics and doctors and nurses who worked on me. The SWAT team and first responders. I wouldn't be walking all over the city without them."

"Are you thinking of a career change? A third Daubman doctor?"

"Oh, fuck, then I'd be like my sisters," I said. I want to believe my sisters mean well, that each followed a higher calling to heal others, do no harm, and such, but I don't believe that. I saw their race to doctor-hood as status-climbing and badge-collecting. I don't think they really care about their work. They care about how other people care about their work.

"Then, what?" Abby asked.

Just as the body inflames and walls off areas of trauma to heal itself, so, too, does the mind. Despite our best, or worst efforts, the two, body and mind, steadily strive toward wholeness.

"Big Brothers/Big Sisters. I downloaded an application."

"Kids?"

"For short periods at a time. We take one in for a few hours, we give her back."

"You get the application started," Abby said. "You're right. There's nothing inevitable about how we're living. We can change whatever we want."

"Necessary. Nothing necessary."

Outside on the deck, stillness. Hints of morning light nudge forward. In Ohio, I never paid the sky much attention. Abby had. She'd sit on her balcony and gaze into cloud formations. I'd tease her that watching the sky wasn't much different than watching paint dry.

"Behind all that stillness," she'd say, "the sky is alive and breathing. It's vast and endless and connects us all around the world. Everyone has a sky to stare at, a sky that goes on for miles."

"Skies are different," I said. "Different pollutions. Think of L.A. at four in the afternoon, all that traffic. Or Beijing. Their sky is deadly."

"The sky is new canvas every day."

"Careful, you sound like a mystic."

The Seattle sky is different than the Ohio sky. In Ohio, the sky flows with light, jubilant blues even in winter. Here, yes, of course there's light, but it's always filtered through a gray so heavy that breathing becomes a labor. Somehow, though, we trust that winter always lays plans for spring.

I am alone and accompanied. Each house I pass holds its own large and small tragedies. Year after year, inhabitants continue to shoot rockets and fireworks, hold parties and ceremonies, string lights, put up trees and sad plastic reindeer. They preserve their rituals and empty habits. The neighbor sounds an air horn after Sunday touchdowns. Meanwhile, the Wilsons, a block over, lost a daughter eight months ago. She collapsed on the basketball court from a quiet heart defect that erupted at age fifteen. Behind the Wilson's house a thirteen-year-old rigged his dad's shotgun to pull a string and blow his own head off. Consider the thought and planning. A strong string, the right angles, perfect-enough physics. Four streets over, a wife, a writer who published several books, has Alzheimer's. Up the road, oxygen warning signs in the windows. Marie has pulmonary fibrosis, the third sibling of three, all diagnosed at sixty-seven, the first two dead by seventy-two. And in the blue house with the gray trim surrounded by a wild yard live two women, one of whom suffered trauma in a school massacre.

I remember the oxymora lesson in sophomore English. Deafening silence. Christian soldier. Hell's Angels. Living dead. Seriously funny. The class of fifteen-year-olds laughed at the truths that sprung from the wordplay. Consciousness of the absurdity around us and the hypocrisy to follow seeped into our questioning minds. School massacre, even school shooting, tops them all. Massacre itself is an ugly word best reserved for wars and acts of terror in foreign places. Massacre. Overused. Commonplace. Another awful form of adaptation. People get used to anything.

I take night walks to silence myself.

I take these walks to retrain my muscles. Build up the right quad, right gluteals, hamstrings. Many days these muscles refuse to initiate, their circuitry shorted. So I drag my leg, near dead weight, along behind me.

What matters?

There is always another day. Another way to tell the story, to feel, to shape my life, one foot, the other, one choice, another. Acknowledge the ache and keep limping forward. Toward what? Doesn't matter. People survive. This is our purpose. Some go on to do great things, most don't. We try to stand upright and walk in the right direction, but gravity's relentless pressure bows us.

All of that is behind us now. We sit here, sometimes alone, sometimes together, answering your questions. I heard your thesis had to do with dreams. In my recurring dream, I'm driving to meet Abby. I'm on an on-ramp, and I can't merge into traffic. Car after car whizzes past. I sit with the engine idling, alternately pressing the gas and the brake. I can't move. I'm cemented at the top of the ramp. My dreams have never been so obvious.

BETTERMENT

Four decades ago, my wife was in foster care for three years. She used to mention it on occasion, but mostly didn't like to talk about it. Usually she'd talk about anything, but on the topic of foster care, she stayed quiet. Even when David, her foster brother, showed up, she didn't say much. And they certainly didn't reminisce in mixed company. David used to pop in when things ended. Jobs, relationships, TV shows. "Things have gone fucky again," he'd say and flop onto our couch, all melodrama and lankiness. As much as I loved David in my have-to-tolerate-him-because-he's-family way, I hated that Abby accommodated him. Of course, I was infinitely, if not morbidly, curious about what had gone on between them in that foster home, but I never asked, feigning respectful distance. If Abby had moved on, I didn't need to be the one moving her back.

I was in diapers when Abby and David were teenagers. She could have been my babysitter. Cougar that she is, she still refers to me as her special friend. And she is my old lady. Finally. When we first met, Abby had said we could have a fling and that was all. "A little fun for a little while. Thirteen years is a whole generation," she said by way of argument.

"A lifetime," I agreed.

"Yes," she said in one of our many post-coital conversations when we were defenseless, sated, and comfortably exposed. "You're a Smith grad. You know the probabilities of things like this. They never work out."

"Smith equals liberal arts, well-rounded think-about-anything-and-everything for four years. You're mistaking it for MIT where real math takes place."

"I'm sure they teach the same statistics at both institutions."

"But not how they're used."

She teased me about Smith, perhaps envious that I spent my college days among experimenting, anarchist-minded coeds who wanted as many conquests as their male compatriots at other schools. I had notched my share, most of them short-sighted in hypothesis and design, and all of them failed. I liked my girls older.

"Old, you mean."

"Semantics."

A little fun for a little while. I knew better. I knew from the beginning. The funding dried up. The experiments ended.

The beginning. My birthday. Akihiro. Translation: bright and large. I'd looked into the etymology at some point. I met my large glory at Akihiro, down on lower Vine. Abby's role at the restaurant involved wrangling Akihiro's three petulant sons into preparing menu items instead of trying to best one another's plates in their private game of next best chef. Mostly, Abby sat in the upstairs office behind three panes of glass overlooking the restaurant floor. She ordered supplies, scheduled staff, maintained ledgers, and completed crossword puzzles when she wasn't up to corralling the boys to their stations. She could complete the *New York Times* Friday puzzles but rarely the weekend challenges. The restaurant was a success, so Abby's job wasn't hard, although she did have the unfortunate task, infrequent as it was, of escorting the occasional belligerent patron out the door, which is how we met.

Rebecca, a friend from Northampton, was drunk and irate on arrival to my birthday. Several days before, I'd told her we couldn't have sex any more. While not a Smith student, Rebecca had trolled the Smith campus with undeterred regularity. A quad fixture my freshman year, she could be found hacky-sacking or tossing a Frisbee in any weather. She was the organizing force behind rugby-style Ultimate games, meaning full body contact always. We met officially when she rolled me into a giant puddle during spring midterms week. Then she appeared outside my classes. At first I thought she'd been there all along, like a drinking fountain I'd passed a hundred times without succumbing to its rusty taste. Rebecca fessed quickly that she had friends in the registrar's office through whom she had filched my schedule.

"Stalking is a form of flattery, I suppose."

"You bet it is," she said. "I'm glad you see it that way."

Rebecca dropped out her sophomore year, preferring to smoke pot, have sex, and occasionally work odd jobs rather than sit at a desk and prove herself on exams. After her third appearance outside my business admin class, we became inseparable in my free time, and cordially non-monogamous for the next three years. Upon my graduation and acceptance to graduate school, Rebecca followed me to Cincinnati. Our habit was to fuck a couple times per month, but she soiled this arrangement by shooting heroin. She insisted the needle was clean and that she'd only done it for a one-time experience, but one dirty needle changes a life irrevocably. I cared too much about my own health, and hers, to trust her choices. In Massachusetts, I'd had to take her to the ER more than once after several hours of nonstop vomiting from too many pills mixed with too much alcohol. Rebecca had no off switch, no internal governor to limit her velocity. At Akihiro she got loud and physical, her voice shrill, her arms flailing. Her fourth sake made her belligerent. When she started slamming things against the table, the manager came forward and asked us to leave. Cue the golden light and Abby's slow-motion approach.

"I'm sorry for my friend," I said, ushering Rebecca out the door while looking back at the manager, slender and strong and about six inches taller than I was. I couldn't look away. I didn't want to leave. "My name's Liz."

"Great, just keep moving."

"What's yours?"

My four years of failed experiments did yield unabashed confidence. I didn't agonize over someone's sexuality. I went back to Akihiro the next day and asked the manager out for a drink. As for the sexuality puzzle, at a bar that evening, Abby grazed my knee with her hand more than once, and then rested her hand three inches above my knee, owning me forever in that single gesture. "Would you like to come home with me?" she asked. Directness made all transactions so much easier. We started having sex that first night, life being short and all, and waiting its own theatre of the absurd. Three hours is enough to stir magic and create longing and know whether to invest more time. For all her quiet reserve, Abby was firm and vocal about her wants. "Reservations in the bedroom are a waste of time," she said. I hadn't known until that moment how much I agreed.

We spent a lot of that February indoors. Snow and sleet compelled us. A nasty winter. Who am I kidding? Her body compelled me. Her movements charged me. Caught in the psychosis of early love, I didn't want to leave her bed, and she was complicit in keeping me there. However, by May we rejoined the world, slowly, by taking walks in Eden Park, around the concrete pond and water towers, through the observatory and museum. A springtime blur of sunshine and radiant energy drew us closer. Abby had memberships to museums. We walked the galleries, our feeble way of supporting the arts. I said we were maintaining the cultural balance and that museum-going was better than watching sports any day. "All professional athletes should have salary caps. Anything over a million a year should be recycled into social programs and cleaning up the country. The amount of money, creativity, and intelligence that goes into professional sports is obscene. Think of what America would look like if we made better use of our resources."

"Norway. It would look like Norway," she said.

"But then there's the far side of art. Rebecca and I went to an Edward Hopper retrospective in New York one weekend. We were supposed to have a weekend of high culture—museums, a Broadway show, some lesser-known off-Broadway play, high tea and French cuisine."

"But instead?"

"We ended up at a body mutilation party. All these people dressed in reds and black, leather, metal, dark eye make-up. And the noise! Loud dissonant industrial noise."

"Some might call that music."

"That's a stretch. The finale involved slipping giant hooks through skin near the shoulder blades and hoisting people to the ceiling as if they were naked angels suspended in air."

"What were they after?"

"No idea, but the whole deal was scary and fascinating and not a little unsanitary. There was blood, after all, and not enough latex to go around. Rebecca's always been an extremist. She dabbled with rough sex so I'm not surprised she found that venue and wiggled her way into the after-party. She was hung over the next day, so I went to a Barnett Newman showing on my own and was blown away. You'd like Newman. He's very austere, yet overwhelming. Suffocating and free at the same time."

"The zips. I know his work. Hopper and Newman are polar opposites on the surface, except that Newman's work is painful to look at, physically, I mean. A hook to the insides."

"A sharp hook to the soul."

"Both study empathy. True empathy, suffering *with*."

"Yes," I said. Oh, how she surprised me.

"You haven't found my secret stash. My books in the closet."

Oh, how she titillated me.

When she listened, Abby rarely interrupted. She maintained soft and appropriate eye contact. I wanted her to know everything. I wanted to be known by her. Confirmed in the world. In *her* world. I told her everything from the beginning. The standard and ubiquitous coming-out story. My taste in music and theatre. Two semesters of rampant masturbation. Violin practice. Practice with boys. My dabble in the Spoken Wyrd Riots. NYC weekends and polyamory. She lacked my need for confirmation. Hence my attraction. She had nothing to prove and thus no impulse to prove it. Ambition and angst soften with age. I hadn't softened yet.

Compared to my peers, I had a late sexual awakening. I didn't orgasm until I was twenty. Alone and reading a book in my dorm room, I put my hand down my pants and mindlessly twirled over my nob while my roommate was off somewhere beneath her boyfriend. My peers encountered sex at fifteen, sixteen, seventeen, with even some unmolested, consent-giving outliers at thirteen and fourteen. By contrast, I floundered twice in high school with shy boys. I'd wanted more and felt left out of mainstream rites of passage, but didn't know how to engage in them either. Sophomore year of college, though, proved a blur and frenzy. First semester, fingers down my pants rubbing the button raw any chance I could—library stacks, bathrooms, between classes. Second semester, I turned outward and rubbed others. After a thousand hours of practice, I could make any girl come in my hand. That's why I wasn't successful in high school. I'd been trying the door to the wrong world.

Because she kept listening, smirking and nodding, encouraging me, Abby got to hear about my experiments.

Initial scientific query: How many discrete women can one woman have sex with within one seven day period? Nota bene: discrete is not to be confused with discreet.

Hypothesis: The reasonable assumption is seven, one per day.

Design: Sequential case series. Have sex with as many women by any consensual means necessary.

Operational definition(s): Sex, as understood in this study, is a broad and inclusive term, not limited to intercourse or penetration. Too sad and unimaginative, those categories. What counts as sex, with and/or without the use of toys or other implements? Touching, kissing, smiling, talking, grinding, fucking, fucking, fucking, finger-fucking, ass-fucking, tongue-fucking, biting, breathing, sighing, laughing, rolling, scissoring, mouthing, licking, tickling, nippling, clamping, and any and all permutations thereof. Additional requisite: at least one of the participants in each event must orgasm.

Discussion: The results of this study are limited by the researcher's extraneous school and work obligations. Huge impediments, those.

Conclusion: Nine.

Second study, initial query: How many women can one woman have sex with at one time?

Hypothesis: Assuming all parties are without handicap or disability, with full use of mouths, tongues, both hands, moderately adept with toys, five. This also assumes use of a standard hotel room with a king-sized bed.

Design: Your basic oversized orgy.

Operational definition(s): See aforementioned study.

Discussion: Think octopuses. Tentacles and appendages and suckers. Arms and legs and tongues reaching, probing, thrashing, searching, failing, sucking, pushing, accepting. In reality the matrix is more like a chain-linked fence. I fuck her as she fucks her who licks her who kisses her who rims her who jams her left hand into her whose forearm muscles spasm, forcing a rest and a reconfiguring.

Result: No one is attended to fully, and everyone leaves unsated.

Conclusion: Inconclusive. While large numbers are theoretically possible, finding even four persons willing to participate is untenable under these experimental conditions. Dina Shore, Mardi Gras, Burning Man, and the Michigan Womyn's Fest may yield more successful recruitment and a far more consequential study.

Closing remark: Don't bother.

Some would label my experiments post-feminist adventures in Erica Jongian fictional sex queendom. Others would call me a slut. Fired by seize-the-day, know-and-own-your-body, and power-to-the-cunt mindsets, I experienced all I could while I could. Between twenty and twenty-five, there's no justification for monogamy. I could settle when the time came. Abby had her own history, of course, but not one as copious as mine. Her limited history, however, did not lack for adventure. A performance artist was once involved, not to mention Abby's appearance for an on-stage episode of fisting.

"You'd never know it was me," she said. "I wore a black gown with a hood and green latex gloves. There were several single mattresses stacked up with a green oval, a ball—a pea, between two of them. Margot was no princess. She was not effecting change. I don't know that art can, especially fringe art. And think of the audience for those shows. People who already sit far left of anything reasonable. That, or groundlings."

"Art can do more than we think. Remember when Ellen came out on her show and kissed whatshername, that skinny blond? Sure, the show got cancelled and sponsors dropped their ads and other backlash, but look what followed. *Will & Grace*, the lezzie wedding on *Friends*, the granddaughter in *Parenthood*, the bisexual mother in *Two and ½ Men*. *Modern Family*. *Glee*. There are loads of queer characters in shows. Ellen opened the door and now she's billionaire successful. People love her. Middle America loves her."

"You know way too much about TV, which, by the way, is a different beast than the back alley stage."

"Margot *did* make a name for herself."

"She did, it's true, but my hand in my girlfriend's cunt was pure spectacle. Spectacle and shock is all it is."

"Art takes many forms. The personal *is* wildly political. You opened a window on alternative realities. You know you agree on some small level. Otherwise you'd never have taken part. You fisted someone onstage! That's a story for the grandkids."

"We're not having kids."

I didn't need to win the discussion. I was happy Abby had started using *we* on occasion. "Why green gloves?" I asked.

"Who knows anymore?"

Drawn to the artist-type, Abby had dated the spectrum— poet, painter, musician. A dancer who moved to NYC then to Vegas and whom until eight months into our relationship, she still saw from time to time. She briefly saw a sculptor who wanted kids, which meant a hard-stop to the relationship. There were a few other dalliances that Abby dismissed with a wistful brush of her fingertips along her bottom lip.

"Artful pornography," she explained, "nothing more than artful pornography. Margot went west after that run. The thing about artists is they're incredibly selfish and passionate. They're volatile. Being around them makes life feel so much more real and awake and meaningful."

"No Flaubert in the bunch? Keeping their lives boring and routine?"

"Not a one, which may explain their mediocrity. And narcissistic. Did I mention the narcissism?"

"You fed on their energy."

"Sure," she allowed, "when I was younger."

"And now?"

"You're not playing at art, are you?"

"I pluck at the cello every so often."

"Which means it doesn't consume you. Musicians are a different breed anyway. Now I read and look at art. I don't try to live with the artist. Instead, I support from a distance like a parent helping pay for college."

Not awkward, not pained, and not amused, Abby, misfit to any bar scene, on a short handful of occasions stood to the side near the jukebox or sat on a stool while I danced with friends or yelled through the music about nothing important. In our early days, I had endless capacity for nights without substance. Abby had endless irritation for the same. Not shy nor uncomfortable, she simply didn't like breezy social interactions. They annoyed her because she didn't see their point. She'd rather stay home with a worthwhile book or movie or sit on the balcony, watching the night descend, listening to birdsong and city sirens. A quiet life. I was learning to like it.

Rebecca, opposite, extroverted, abhorrent of introspection, always up for out-ness, chatting and dancing wherever and with whomever, and having settled into screwing someone else, invited us out all the time. Usually I declined, but occasionally I still needed a night out. When I coerced Abby, on a full moon a year into our relationship, to go out with my friends, she said, "I suppose we should meet each other's people."

We met Rebecca and a few others across the river at the Crazy Fox. Seeing me enter, Rebecca dropped her darts and embraced me. Whatever passed between us, whatever was going on, whatever happy or sour mood she was in, Rebecca was always enthusiastic for a hug, one in which you felt held, contained, and loved, if not by the world at large, then at least in her world.

With her arms tight around me, her electric, warm body against mine, Rebecca breathed into my ear, "She's old, Lizzy."

"Thirteen years is nothing."

"Thirteen years is *old* pussy."

"You're jealous," I said.

"Of old pussy? Not in the least." She still held me. "What does she do?"

"I told you, she runs the restaurant you got us kicked out of a year ago." We broke from the clutch. Rebecca pursed her lips, judgment festering. "Don't start," I said. "What are *you* doing?"

"Living, Liz, experiencing everything. Every. Thing. Last week I did a special tour in Mammoth Caves. Ever been there?" I had, having grown up two and a half hours from there, but she didn't wait for my answer. "In Kentucky? I met this guy, Jeff, a couple weeks ago. He's an anarchist artist. He likes to paint or draw or put up well-known pieces in weird places. Like, he'll put Mona Lisas in truck stop bathroom stalls or he'll pepper library stacks with Campbell soup can stickers. So, we're in the caves and he takes out some pink chalk from his pocket and starts sketching animals on the walls. You know like the ones in France?"

"It's so meta," Abby said. I could hear the deviousness in her tone, and a rare and feisty mood. "But anarchistic? It's quite fitting—illegal, of course, but at least he was kind enough to use chalk."

Rebecca stared at Abby, not quite sure what to say.

"Now, if he'd put Hello Kitty on the walls or Barbie, that would be interesting. Still using chalk, of course. But where's the anarchism, the Courbet? Art, as he said, should show the lives of working people and all the shit they go through because they're at the mercy of the upper classes."

"He's free. That's the point. He's in the camp that chases after what it wants. No patrons, no modern art world," Rebecca said. "But anyway, afterward he went to New York for some project. Then a couple days ago this boi, Ande, and I tripped balls at Kings Island. On Thursdays I go to The Box for the ropes demo. They always need consenting bodies. Last week we worked on suspensions."

"Like a trapeze artist."

Rebecca ignored Abby, the old pussy. "I'm still after *it*, Liz, ultimate experience. You used to want to experience all of *it*. You used to think the same way. What the fuck? You're nine-to-five in *data management*. When did you become so boring?"

"I've always been boring," I said, which wasn't necessarily true. I didn't feel bored or that I was a boring person during my time with Rebecca, nor did I feel that way with Abby. On the contrary, with Abby I felt whole and free and overwhelmed all to various degrees. "I've always been pragmatic. Take the lit and the philosophy and art classes *and* the economics, business, and computer programming ones. I studied at college and now I have a job at the university hospital. Some people follow through on the things they start."

"Head in the clouds, feet on the ground," she said.

"Head below the clouds and feet on the ground," I corrected.

"And that one?" Rebecca asked pointing to Abby, who was at the bar, getting drinks. "What gives with that?"

"I'm experiencing monogamy and intimacy now."

"Jesus."

"I'm home, Rebecca."

"With a manager? Good luck with that."

Abby could have pursued bigger or more vital things, had she wanted. She knew a little bit about a lot. She didn't feel compelled to perfect herself in the world. She was well-read and cultured. She understood my esoteric jokes and could tell ones of her own. She knew what it meant, fourteen months in, when I sent her a copy of *Love, Death, and The Changing of the Seasons* with a tab on page 21: *here, this. You*, which prompted a text:

> *Have you read all of it?*
> *You DO know how the story ends?*

I replied:

> *A little fun for a LONG while.*
> *Love, Death, and The Changing of Season*
> *after Season after Season, after. . .*
> *I am young and energized.*

I was hovering, circling, homing pigeon that I was. Abby remained herself and kept to her routines. She knew how to be separate. I was familiar with co-dependency and jealousy and heartache, co-eds finding and losing themselves on dad's dimes. Abby, ever levelheaded and assertive about solitude, carried no guilt. "Relationships only last if individuals maintain their individuality."

"So we're in a relationship?"

"No need to be exclusive. Just let me know if we need to be practicing safe-ish sex."

I, of course, had been exclusive from the beginning. I'd had none better, nor could I imagine anyone else supplanting Abby.

"And you, Rebecca?" Abby asked, passing drinks around. "Are you home?"

"I'm home everywhere, lady. Wherever this body is, there I am. Free."

"The first human ever."

"Meaning?"

"No one's free. We're all products and bi-products. Language traps us. Society, media, advertising, culture."

"You found yourself a deep one, Liz. As for me, I sleep where I want, fuck who I want. I don't punch a clock or have to *manage* anything."

"Like a teenager," Abby said.

"Fuck no. Yeah. Whatever. I'm having a blast. That's all that matters."

Rebecca collected a quiver of darts from the floor. The bar filled and lines formed for drinks and pinball. I looked at Abby and watched the playful extrovert disappear. She'd maxed out on sociability, and would soon excuse herself. She'd tell me to have fun. She'd see me later that night or later in the week. No matter what I said or tried, she would not be cajoled into doing something she did not want to do. Abby's need for time alone didn't feel selfish, nor did I feel any less wanted. I learned quickly that solitude redoubled her ardor. Absence not only made our hearts fonder but our sex better. That night she fucked any sheen of Rebecca right off of me.

Ever amused and annoyed by Abby's relationship with me, David came and went when he wanted, as he pleased. *His* absences didn't make me fonder of him. Substitute siblings, each other's witness, Abby, eleven to fourteen, David, thirteen to sixteen, he was the first to know she got her period. She watched him pierce his eyebrow, then watched his dad rip it out. He was her first kiss among other gropings she doesn't discuss. I can only imagine David stinky from skateboarding, masturbating in front of her, proudly displaying his well-handled manhood, or him licking the skin fold between her thigh and labia because any further center made him, at that age, think he'd taste pee. Penetration? They must have had sex with condoms stolen from his dad's bedside drawer. Teen thrusting with socks and shirts on. Parents, out bowling, drinking at bars, leaving the kids alone too long. I liked David less the more I thought about him.

Abby's Rebecca was David.

My dislike started when I was on my hands and knees, shifting sometimes fast, sometimes slowly, as Abby, strapped in, fucked me from behind, a position at the time I wanted at least twice weekly. Abby was always happy to oblige.

A voice from the doorway: "So this is your new dog."

I'd been walked in on in college, but those sightings ended in a flash with an embarrassed voyeur dashing away. David, hardly. He rooted, unabashedly spooning yogurt into his face. I'd also found myself in situations where unsure but curious women wanted only to watch. I'd learned to focus on the sensations of my body without concern for spectators. I was surprised, though, by Abby. Her thighs grazed mine, pulled away, grazed, left. Keeping this rhythm, she said, "Oh, fuck, that's David. I'll introduce you later. David, you're excused. You can make make yourself at home as always, just not in my bedroom doorway right this minute. In fact, if you'd close the door behind you, please, and give us some privacy?"

He delayed too long before doing as asked. David closed the door, and Abby still thrusting, said, "This is what the rest of your life comes with."

"It's almost enough to force a pass."

When David arrived from Chicago, Abby neglected Pilates or skipped work to eat with him—things she rarely did for me. With his own key, David arrived and left, any time of year, at all times of day and night. On one visit, he arrived unannounced to find me naked in the kitchen, retrieving coffee. And while Abby and I weren't living together, we spent weekends in her apartment where I felt at ease. David appraised me, and said, "Yeah, okay, I can see why she's keeping you around. Just look at that taut little behind."

"A simple hello is sufficient. Abby!" I yelled. "David is here." He and I never bothered with a conversation of any depth or value. We held to an unspoken pact of mutual tolerance. I slowly sunk the plunger of the French press. Abby emerged from the bedroom. She was dressed and handed me a robe, then kissed David on the cheek, asking him why the frequency of his visits had suddenly increased.

"Another relationship soured. Had to blow out of the windy city."

I suspected he was testing my resilience, trying to drive me away so he could have Abby to himself again.

"You're still here?" he asked sometime later.

"Leave her alone, David."

"You know I'm only kidding."

"Are you?" I said and disappeared into the bedroom. I'd taken to silent, solitary reading whenever he talked to Abby about how young I was, asking her how long she planned to play with me. "You've had young," she accused. "*Had*," he replied.

David had been teaching in Chicago and living part-time with an older man who refused to divorce his wife of twenty-some years. David's irritation divided him between his love for Abby, his need to be her first priority, and the fact that he felt like the younger, neglected one in his relationship. David didn't compromise well, or at all, unless he was forced to. Abby enforced a nine-day limit on his stays. I advocated for five. She would have settled at fourteen.

With respect to monogamy, David wanted it from Charles, his lover, but would never submit to it himself. "Why commit? There are so many penises and vaginas in the world to be experienced! What possible argument could there be for monogamy? In the non-human animal world, it's almost unheard of. We are not chimps, after all. We're bonobos."

Yet all rules have exceptions. David's exception was Charles. My guess was, had Charles left his wife, David would have dropped everything and run to him. Instead, David used non-monogamy as a defense mechanism.

Sometime in the third year Abby and I were together, clanging and laughter resounded in the kitchen.

"David, what are you doing?" Abby yelled as she charged from the bed. She pulled a robe on in a huff. "It's fucking three a.m."

"Where is your booze, Abigail my love? Meet Bianca. She's from the Ukraine, studying—what are you studying, doll?"

"Russian literature."

"Imagine that. She came all this way to study her neighbors. Isn't she a gorgeous piece of androgyny? All angles and accents."

"David, your travel visa was up five days ago."

He rolled his eyes. "Nine days is so arbitrary."

"We've talked about this."

"My Russian Clit, you'll have to come home with me to Chicago."

I met Abby at the halfway point of her life. The rest downhill, or so they say. She didn't see things the way I did, however. "When I met you, I felt like I was just beginning." This she told me on our second anniversary. "I felt like I'd arrived home." Out for dinner one night, near the end of year three, Abby put her hand on my thigh well above my knee. "Would you like to live together?"

She was not easy to live with at the start. At forty-seven, she was established, had set her surroundings. Except for occasional girlfriends and David's sleepovers, she'd lived alone for over a decade. Everything of hers had its place and she her routines. Dishes cleaned, dried, and put away after each meal. Laundry on Thursdays. Austere artwork—black and white photographs only—would be hung with a level. Though I was the librarian (library scientist!), she relished quiet more than I did. Sunday mornings *New York Times* and *This American Life*, classical music or jazz. My ears ached, but I got over restlessness. I stopped blasting Ani DiFranco and Melissa Ferrick, and I reserved Sleater Kinney for nights when Abby took to the restaurant. I overcame youthful tastes because Abby looked good—lithe and strong and seductive, without trying. That's probably why she was so seductive. She was unaware of her impact on others. And she did take care. Trimmed and well-manicured, she visited the sugarer twice monthly and kept to Pilates three times weekly. We met on my thirtieth birthday.

Abby and I lived separately and dated for four years, a record in lesbian annals. A wedding invitation and note from Rebecca arrived during Abby's and my first year of living together. Rebecca's third round of rehab had apparently flipped her neural circuitry. She'd been sober for more than a year. She'd met Rachel in AA or NA or some other A. She was living in Ann Arbor, planning for a ceremony in one of the metro parks, followed by a honeymoon at the Michigan Womyn's Music Festival. She wanted me as a witness, if not her BestBest, her gender-neutral term for maid of honor and best man.

At the wedding, Rebecca's head was shaved short around the sides and back, and her hair, long, dyed black, spiked omni-directionally on top. She wore a dog collar for a bow tie and black Birkenstocks. Rachel, elegant in a blue-gray lace bodice crepe gown, presented herself as a more traditional bride, except for her yarmulke and full right-sleeve and left-stirrup pant-leg tattoos of trendy fish and ripped-off Hokusai images. For the ceremony, chairs had been arranged in five triangles forming a star. In the center of the star was a plain tall purple table with a contract on it. Rebecca and Rachel walked separate oblique aisles to the table.

Rachel said, "Do you?"

"Yes," Rebecca replied. "Do you?"

"Yes."

They each signed the contract, and the ceremony/performance piece was over. The reception commenced. As recovering addicts, the brides made the reception dry. This was unfortunate because their guests stood around awkwardly, making small talk, glasses of mineral water in hand, while the brides danced and walked around to each person handing out lit candles and too-intimate kisses. Their cake, which they refused to smash into each other's faces—such a gesture deemed too violent and degrading—was gluten-free, dairy-free, and refined sugar-free. At one point Rebecca pulled me aside, thanked me for coming, and made her amends. She even apologized to Abby for the night in the restaurant.

The fact that Rebecca had known Rachel for a far shorter amount of time than Abby and I had been together made several people ask if we were going to hold a ceremony and exchange vows.

"Unlikely," Abby said.

"Yes," I said.

Neither of us bothered to elaborate.

In sum, the day was odd and discomfiting, and the wedding a strange political freak show. At its end, I was all too glad to be alone in a hotel room with Abby. She had gone down to use the hot tub, had come back and showered. After she'd dried off, she propped her foot on the bed and caressed lotion into her legs. "Are you sorry you came?" I asked, not taking my eyes off her. For eons, I could watch her hand glide up her leg.

"It was amusing," Abby said. "I've seen worse."

"I find that hard to believe," I said, still watching her. She was in no hurry. "Should we marry?"

"This again?"

"The laws are changing. We could go to Iowa."

"Then we'd be in Iowa."

"You're it for me, Ab. Be my DP. Marry me."

"I've sat through enough weddings, more than my fill for a lifetime. They're boring, and I don't say that about a lot of things. And today's? There wasn't a truly sacred moment. It was a farce. A studded dog collar? I mean seriously. Besides, I don't want to subject family and friends to the chicken dance and gluten-free cardboard cake. I don't require a ring or a contract to confirm what I feel."

Even I found the dog collar too much, and I loved anyone who soiled tradition. And there was something to Rebecca's demeanor throughout the day that I didn't quite trust. The word lobotomized kept coming to mind. With the exception of her outfit, Wedding Rebecca was not Northampton Rebecca nor the Rebecca that used to pull me into threesomes, or public bathrooms. She was not the Rebecca who used to do shots off people's bellies or slip her hand down my pants in movie theatres. I suppose I was feeling protective of her, she being the one woman I'd been with the most often until Abby. Rebecca had lodged a special nostalgic adhesion in my heart. Despite their smiles and surreptitious groping, Rebecca and Rachel were not long for each other, or so I thought.

Abby, though, surprised me. Weddings as sacred? She rarely talked religion or God and had several atheist books on her shelves. Anytime discussions of the afterlife came up, she'd say, "Worry about the afterlife when you're in the afterlife. Try living this life" or "the burden of proof is on them," referring to religious believers. I hadn't thought of it that way, steeped as I was in my family's brand of Catholicism. I'd long since stopped believing and had stopped observing holy days and sacraments. I wasn't ashamed of the type of Catholicism my parents practiced. They didn't agree with eighty percent of Catholic Doctrine, but they liked the rituals and smell of incense and the Jesuit emphasis on knowledge and social justice. A family trip to Rome and the Vatican steered them further left. They didn't like the decadence and being shunted like cattle through the holy halls. After that we spent Thanksgivings in soup kitchens, passed out sleeping bags and socks in the winter. My mom always had a trunk full of pop-top food cans, plastic sporks, and a napkin for corner beggars. My dad wasn't opposed to buying a guy a beer in exchange for his story. My parents were involved, engaged socially and set a strong example of how to lead a moral life.

In the hotel, when Abby had finished her moisturizing ritual, she came close and let her towel drop to the floor. "I'm fully committed to you, Liz," she said and took hold of my head in her strong hands and kissed me. "You don't doubt that, do you?" Then she guided my hand high between her legs. Just about all of Abby's reluctance, I knew, came directly from her childhood with its repeated early lessons in abandonment. Whatever other reason there was was theoretical, political, historical. However, marriage as an institution, an ancient one at that, with its emphasis on making alliances, expanding the family work force, its strict roles, property exchange, and other arrangements and agreements, was dead. And in June 2015, gays and lesbians in the United States could marry, legally, federally. Ten years after Canada and Spain, nine years after South Africa, a year after Britain, five years after parts of Mexico, and a full two plus decades after Denmark and Norway. The list goes on.

I didn't doubt Abby's commitment. Not at all.

After eight years, Rebecca finally stopped referring to Abby as old pussy, David stopped outwardly objecting to our relationship, and Abby confessed to wanting "a little more than a little fun." She dropped her job, her apartment, her easy visits from David, her disdain for marriage, and moved west with me when I accepted a job in Seattle, consulting on data mining and management. This is what an MLS can get you— a lifetime of cubicles, computers, and code in a tech-heavy, rain-sodden city. We bought a house with a water view. We had drinks with our neighbors. We voted yes to greenbelts and education and no to stadiums and ripping out old trees for new construction. We bought a Subaru and a Prius. We tried hot yoga and yoga in the park in the rain and ate at sustainable sushi restaurants. We were happy and my head was high. The clouds were nines, lined silver when we wedded at the courthouse, settling firmly in to a new city, living our cozy, dignified, adult, and married lives.

IMPEDIMENT

In addition to my full-time position in data management, I consulted for small town schools, guiding their libraries into the digital age. I liked the travel, dropping into big cities and driving out of them to farm country or factory suburbs where life slowed and people aged better. They had tighter communities. Citizens' votes made a difference in small towns. Stoplights were erected, snow removed and ice broken up, curfews lifted, sidewalks widened, trees planted. Small-town people had time for hellos and gossip, bake sales and town meetings. Fewer eyes seem trained on phones. Small towns warped time, and made me feel afloat in limbo. That torpidity was a welcomed interruption to beige cubicles, Seattle gloom, and computer screens. Before that, the work I'd done in Cincinnati transpired in an administrative wing near the medical college library. I oversaw a team preparing for a major diagnostic code change, ICD-9 to 10. The United States, as usual, lagged behind the rest of the world in converting—a full decade behind some countries.

The town of Rookwood, Colorado, had seen significant growth with the surprise addition of a large data storage facility and a few small but growing tech companies. The latest batch of computer programming CEOs liked the snow and ski of Colorado. Rookwood High School graduated fifty-seven in 2016 and was projected to matriculate three-hundred into its senior class by 2020. Room sat empty awaiting the growth. At Rookwood, I'd finished for the day, shook hands with the librarian and principal, latched my case. I thought I might get a ski in before dark. Colorado was snow and endless sun, after all. I had been thinking about my next vacation. It was my turn to choose. The Great Wall? Back to Greece? Lazy beach time in Kauai? Oh, and write up a cooking schedule. I hated cooking, and Abby hated having to be the cook. Compromise. Marriage: a succession of squashed or traded desires. I needed to mow the lawn or plant some hands-free shrubbery. I needed to clean the bathroom and make a Goodwill run. Marriage daily divvied up the chores. That thinking could wait. I might even have time for a post-ski massage. Possibilities everywhere. Death and loss nowhere. The school halls smelled sharply of disinfectant and lemon. The floors gleamed. Proud trophies lined a series of glass cases.

And then.

Pop. Pop.

Fireworks?

Pop. Pop. Pop.

A mishap in chemistry?

Pop. Crack. Pop.

POP. POP.

       Pa. Pa.

Screams. Fast squeaks on glistening tile.

My ears: too much running, pounding, screaming, screeching. Squeak, squeak, squeak, thud, thud. Oh fuck. OH FUCK.

Pop. Pop.

I had wandered aimlessly from the third-floor library.

Poor decision.

My eyes darted and captured gun as my midsection and thigh grew warm, wet. I stumbled and fell and crashed. Over the railing. Stairs and more stairs, as hard as the pain. The noise. Incessant, awful screams—I existed apart from them in a shell of agony. I thought to shout for help. Said it in my mind: help, help, help. Another thought: nature movie advice to play dead. Play. Dead.

Can't move anyway.

I lay dead still amidst footsteps.

I lay and wait. How long? Too long, of course. The waiting. The dull and loud and incessant pain. Liquid. Hot. Cold. Sirens at last cut through the screams and pops and the silences that followed them. I closed my eyes. I gave up. And the sirens led me into . . . .
. . . .
. . . .
. . . .
. . . .
. . . .
. . . . nowhere . . . .
. . . .
. . . . . . .Then blank sounds and thick, loud breath, the glare of monitors, their metronomic beeps. Intense pressure in my throat. So much pressure. So much light. I blinked against the searing light, glimpsed Abby at my side. Abby. My bride.

She has one more surgery. We can't take the tube out yet. I'll have to push more sedation.

Dark silence again.

How long?

Long.

Does it matter?

I gagged back to sentience, panicking, under a thick, full throat. I couldn't swallow. Couldn't breathe. I spasmed panic, certain of the end.

Relax, honey. We'll get that tube out.

Must be the end. No breath. And in my belly—such pain! Snakelike friction in my throat, on my tongue.

Swallow, swallow, breathe.

You're in the hospital. You're okay. Just give me a sec here. I know it feels like you can't breathe, but you are breathing. Don't fight it. Don't force it. The machine is breathing for you.

Heart beat. Beat. Beat. Thumpthumpthump. Abby. At my side. Abby. Look at Abby.

I'm going to take that tube out now. Open your mouth.

Focus on Abby.

A swift slither. No more tube. My throat throbbed and burned. Swallowing felt impossible. My voice croaked charcoal whispers. Again, scorching lights. I blinked. I held my lids closed, but had to look to quell the panic. Nurses and doctors streamed in and out. Always Abby at my side. Her hand on my arm. Her hand on my cheek. Other nurses. The same nurses. Doctors and student doctors. I am a specimen. I am an experiment in gowns and tubes and monitors.

I slept.

An escape. A necessity. I ached through sleep.

We were able to save your leg.
You had a moderate concussion.
Three surgeries in all.
Amazing that the bullet missed bone and artery.
Just a centimeter from your kidney.
Small perforation of your bowel.
Your pelvis caught the worst of it.
You fractured the orbit of your left eye in the fall.
An infection was brewing in your appendix. Took that.
It's a wonder.
A miracle.
You'll walk.
You'll work.
Your life will be normal again.

In addition to the two gunshot wounds and the skull fracture, I'd suffered a dashboard injury. The thighbone smashed into the cup of the pelvis. The acetabulum. I shattered the head of the femur, cracked the cup, and separated the pubic symphysis in the front and the sacroiliac joint in the back. A metal bridge connects my pubic bones. A pin stabilizes my ilium and sacrum. And the bullets, both removed. One shredded the muscle and tissue of my thigh, the other pierced my small intestine.

Abdomens get repaired first to prevent sepsis. Infection with bacteria. Like a septic tank. They removed six inches of intestines. I'll walk, but not for a while. I'll shit normal. Eventually. Once my numbers stabilize and I can pee without a tube, I discharge to a rehab unit to come to terms with my broken body, to try to move forward despite everything, catastrophic everything. At least my bruised face will heal.

Nine days in the ICU.

Eight days on the trauma floor.

At Rookwood High in Nowhere, Colorado, a trio of teens, two boys and a girl, each chose a floor and left forty-two dead and thirty-one injured. The boys shot themselves before SWAT found them. The girl, they potted in the shoulder as she was about to make her own exit. The first female culprit-survivor of a shooting of this magnitude. Before trial and sentencing, she was held in a state psychiatric hospital to recover and be evaluated.

Like me. Held. Monitored. Unlike mine, her ward is locked.

Two weeks in a unit to learn to transfer, with a stapled abdomen and a caged pelvis, from bed to chair, chair to bed, chair to toilet. Fourteen days, then insurance kicks you out. Recover. Such an innocent word.

I learned to shit lying down. I learned to transfer, using only my arms, from bed to chair, chair to shower-bench, then the reverse, an inch at a time. No standing for twelve weeks. Twelve weeks, inch by inch. I learned how time crawled. I learned the limitations of the body. There are so many. And pain. All its scales. 0 to 10. 10 being severe, the worst imaginable. The VAS—visual analog scale. Draw a line between here and here. Run off, nurse, and go measure. The Wong-Baker faces. The smiling face. The crying face. The drunk face. The dumb face. And numb.

Initial resolutions:

> I will be more kind.
> I will learn the piano.

I will pick up the cello again.
I will acquire a second language.
I will express gratitude for daily graces.
I will visit family more often.
I will be kinder to kids and neighbors.
I will live this life better.
Volunteer.
Thanksgiving soup kitchens.
Winter sleeping bags and socks.
I will be a better wife, a better daughter.
Friends came by.

My parents flew in.

Thirty-one days of hospital glare and noise, of strangers checking my pulse, my incisions, asking the day, the president, my name, my birthday, telling me when to sit, lie down, and turn. An entire month.

My sisters, trying to help, arrived from their respective suburbs. They interrogated the doctors, checked my stats.

A few neighbors visited.

The media tried for interviews, and kept trying after everyone else left.

A prepubescent doctor, all thumbs and too much caffeine, plucked the staples from my belly. Thirty-nine staples, one for each of my years, leaving a ribbon of raised red railroad scar. Two days after that, a transport van dropped me home, where, outside the house, three journalists and a TV van awaited me.

Indoors, everything in its place and flowers and fruit bouquets. Strawberries and kiwi, melons and banana. Gerbera daisies, roses, lilies. Splashes of color against Abby's black and white photographs. Elegance and gaud. Part amusing, part pathetic. The firmness had gone out of the table and chairs, the loveseat and cases. The solid house felt fragile, but smelled familiar, flowery, not antiseptic. I sensed Abby watching me as I rolled across the oak floors from room to room. She'd taken up the rugs in preparation for my homecoming. The house now echoed, sounding hollow. Abby could not speak, but I didn't need or want her to. Having her near was enough, and what she held. Facts from the papers. Images from TV. The history of the hospital. Abby. My keeper. Witness through my sleep, my stupor, my anger, my pain.

"Will you light a fire?" I asked.

Abby, my bride. Not until the night I came home did I finally reverse my thinking. *Her* bride. Look at what she's stuck with now: Humpty Dumpty, and a soberly anatomical life to come. I slumped in the hospital-issued wheelchair. I watched dry logs take flame. Abby cleared some books and sat on the coffee table next to me. I clutched her arm and wept.

Soggy and sixty degrees, April in Seattle averaged three inches of rain. The air bit with cold because of the relentless dampness. The sky spread in striated grays across the bay. I couldn't concentrate, couldn't read. My mind drifted. On TV, too much violence. I couldn't handle the news, nor the cacophony of talk radio. I didn't leave the house. I didn't answer the door or phone. I avoided email. Buried in blankets on our back deck, I watched the water. I fought its salty chill. Ferries crossed before me, Fauntleroy to Vashon, Vashon to Fauntleroy. Fauntleroy to Southworth to Vashon. All day, this back and forth. All day the shuttling, A to B, B to A, A to C. Waiting. Shuffling around limbo. Convalescence and crossings. April. Cruelest April. I should have written letters to family and old friends. *Dearest—This summer finds me convalescing on the deck. My pelvis is a wired cage, the miracles of modern medicine!* I didn't write. I didn't call. I watched the ferries chug through their courses hour after hour, all day long, in twenty minute passes from dock to dock. I watched their wake lines, small long hills, run parallel, widen, and disappear. Sixty-plus ferries each day, cutting, re-cutting their swathes. Cargo tankers and small sails crisscrossed the lines, interrupting the monotonous loops.

On land a different loop for me: restless sleep, inch the pelvis along the bed and across the board into a chair, chair to toilet, toilet to chair, lift the rear to dress, lift again, one more time, sweatshirt over the head, gut-pang with the reach. If I didn't move gingerly, I jolted myself into the lower back. To the deck for an hour, to the couch, to the bed. Eat, sleep, dream, drift, shift. A to B, B to A, A to C. Prior to this my medical history had been slight. I hadn't been a sickly child. I wasn't accident-prone. I visited the hospital after my sister had her appendix removed. I was in the ER when my mother's thumb needed stitches. I accompanied Rebecca on her stomach pumps, and I had, as a teenager, had my wisdom teeth removed one afternoon, now a cloaked memory of nitrous fog and drool. At age seven, I broke my arm, then endured a sling and cast and an unbearable itch for several weeks. Medical interactions that were all short bouts. Nothing to prepare me for a siege of trauma, a war against the attrition of my damaged body.

I was not someone who sat still or easily for long, and I was always fiercely independent, which might have sprung from my middle child status, though I didn't feel lost in my family. My parents were diligent about treating their children equally. I don't know if through independence I was trying to differentiate myself from the golden firstborn and the cherished lastborn or if I owed my autonomy to a genetic variation. In a college course, I'd learned about gene mutations, such as the guevedoces in the Dominican Republic, and I wondered whether geneticists would ever isolate the code for lesbianism. If they could figure out how fetal enzyme conversions trigger the growth of genitalia, the discovery of a lesbo gene was surely imminent. In pre-school, I repeatedly tried to pee standing up and ran around without a T-shirt until I turned six, refused to let anyone tie my shoelaces, stubbornly completed all my homework alone, and went to prom solo. Maybe all that was just a behavioral outcome of testosterone dynamics when I was eighteen-weeks formed. I hated how Abby had to aid me and feed me, how she watched me when she adjusted the sliding board and brought blankets to the deck, when she drove me to appointments and held me when I cried, stood aside when I smacked my hands on the armrests or tore at my shirt in frustration. I couldn't stand having a witness to my dependence, to what I'd become.

Good people draw lessons from ill health. They realize all they've taken for granted. After a death skirmish, each day becomes a miracle. The change is genuine, but a defeated brightness radiates from the cancer-crash-AVM-survivor. Good people think about others—the kids, those who died and those who lived, the families. Everyone lost. What becomes of who remain? The kids—will they grow resilient? Defiant? Weak? Will they trust again?

Not one of us survives.

Through those first weeks, conversation with Abby was limited and dedicated to essential tasks:

"Want a shower today or tomorrow?"

"Smoothie or eggs for breakfast?"

"What can I get you from the store?"

"The doctor said you should eat more protein than you normally would."

"Do you remember what normal is?" I asked.

"Is this what old age will be like?" I asked.

"A girl can dream," Abby said, trying for levity. "But our roles will be reversed. I've got more than a decade on you. You'll get to push my thin, wrinkled bag of skin around in a chair and change my Depends. Won't that be a whole new thrill?"

Aging had never bothered me. I welcomed the gathering years because with each one came a little more confidence, a little more love, vacations of increasing comfort, a stronger sense of my place in the world. Aging had also never worried me because the reality remained distant and abstract all through my childhood and adolescence. I wasn't subjected to frail grandparents whose brain vessels blew like land mines, ruining their speech and mobility, nor did they have creeping lung disorders, leaving them breathless and fatigued, nor diabetes to consume their limbs and sight. My grandparents and aunts and uncles did not have lives that dragged on in hospital beds in living rooms before loud TVs. My relatives carried farm-based heartiness from their childhoods into their old age. One grandfather, on the brink of ninety, walked all eighteen holes of the golf course, self-caddying all the way, though frugality alone might have prevented him from renting a cart. And his wife, also in her eighties, took trips every two years with her sister to tour cathedrals and other religious landmarks. I was on the stroke of forty, the mid-life zone of defeat or triumph, the gateway to a new beginning, gray hair and declining metabolism, but all possibilities, good and bad were here now, couched in a barely functioning body. Aging, for the first time, felt daunting.

Sometime in May, we had a physical therapist come to the house. I could have gone to a clinic, but I didn't want to load into the car and unload into an office and repeat. I didn't want Abby driving me to yet more appointments. She'd already shepherded me to follow-up CT scans and MRIs, confirming that my body was healing as it should. Not only did I not want more nursing from Abby, but I also didn't want to spend time with other injured people and their chatter under florescent lights among cheerful staff. I didn't want to share my story. I didn't want to talk at all. The therapist, Tricia, was strong. Her body worked. She had tattoos on the upper third of her arms that teased me with their hints of color and form. She lived in the neighborhood, and I knew I'd seen her at a restaurant or coffee shop, maybe in an advertisement. She exuded a familiar Midwestern sensibility—nice, reserved, with undertones of self-deprecation and dry humor—which all blended into a warm and professional bedside comportment. She was from Ohio and had made her way to Seattle via Alaska and Portland. She was a reader and a bit of a writer and not unpleasant to talk to. She had lived in Fairbanks for three cold years, ostensibly to earn a fine arts degree, but really she said, she was hiking and screwing around. I couldn't see her wasting time. She took her work and me seriously. Imagining her younger and wild required a power of imagination I didn't possess. Plus, she'd had a book published. "A small book of poems. *First Things*," she'd said. "But with patients, I generally don't talk about my writing life."

"Too private?"

"The poems, they're close to my heart, emotionally true, but not biographically. Not factually. Good writing never is. Plus, I wrote those poems a long time ago."

"Poetry *is* fiction."

"Indeed it is. You understand, but most people don't. They mistake fiction for reality, and I wouldn't want my writing to change the way they see me."

"You can't worry about that."

"I have to. I'm in the service-sector. Plus, some of the things I write make *me* uncomfortable."

"Then you're doing something right. Chekov, William Carlos Williams, Conan Doyle. Walker Percy. We all lead multiple lives."

"I don't put myself in their ranks."

"All men. Right. Gertrude Stein! Did you know she did four years of med school and got bored?"

"I know very little about her. Funny thing is I *should* know more about her because the first book, the book of poems is about Alice Austen and Gertrude Tate. Alice and Gertrude. The overlay of names confuses people. I expanded my first book, if you're interested, the expansion and a novel are coming out this year. The Alice poems are now told by Gertrude."

Tricia came to the house on Tuesdays and Fridays to administer physical therapy. At first we practiced sit-to-stand, stand-to-sit, then weight-shifts from foot to foot, side to side, and front to back. I was weak. My body couldn't hold me up, and that set me alight with rage.

"You haven't stood in over eight weeks. You've suffered nerve, muscle, and other tissue damage that's all still repairing itself. We'll do the exercises thirty seconds at a time. Your body will adapt," she said. "Basic training."

"Like the army."

"Sure, if it helps to think that way."

"Why does it hurt when there's so much metal in there?"

"You've been through massive trauma. Your body is adjusting to its new normal. "

"Nothing about this is normal."

"True, your predictable life has been junked. I can't fathom what you've been through."

Unfathomable, yes. I had lived it and even I couldn't believe it.

"Nerves regenerate an inch per month," she continued. "Your body is forming, tearing, and remodeling scar tissue. You're going to feel all kinds of fun and not-so-fun sensations over the next several months."

"Talk to me about something else. Something non-medical. What are you reading?"

"I just finished *The Price of Salt*."

"Terrible."

"You think so?"

"Yes, but it doesn't matter. We all have to read it."

"Check off the lesbians classics."

"I skimmed it, wanting to fast-forward to the sex," I said as she had me stand and sit and sit and stand, distracting me. In time, I came to trust that the floor wasn't going to drop from beneath me. "How'd you like the ending?"

"Cliché nowadays, as happy endings usually are, but I can see why it was revolutionary for its time. Beats the suicides and asylums that normally caught dykes until then."

"The movie was well-done. Understated. Cate Blanchett was smoldering. Speaking of, when can I have sex?"

"Anytime you want. You just can't do it standing up—yet," she said.

"Funny."

After a couple of weeks I could name transitional movements and muscles I didn't know existed. *Iliopsoas. Obturator externus. Obturator internus. Gemellus*—fun to say, that one. Tricia talked in joint mechanics and neuromuscularities. Fascial lines and acupuncture meridians. She told me about proprioception and sarcomeres. I preferred talking books or movies. I looked forward to her visits, which broke up the ferry loops. She had introduced me to Jack Gilbert's poems and some works by others. I still wasn't reading much, but a poem I could manage, if it wasn't too long. Gilbert's had heft instead of length. He'd been married to Linda Gregg and had ditched her for Mishiko, his muse for *The Great Fires*. Then, after Mishiko died, Linda cared for Jack, when he was dying. Those poets and their fierce and convoluted loves!

While I read a line at a time, Abby patrolled the house, consuming an old flame's book cover-to-cover in an afternoon. She sighed as she finished, then went outside on the deck as the sun dropped behind the jagged edges of the Olympic range. I wondered if she wanted Alex, missed her. I wondered if Abby was pissed at our predicament. I didn't ask because I didn't want to know.

When I saw Abby at Akihiro years ago, a sense of inevitability poured through me. Her head was bowed in concentration, unaware of me or others. There was sweetness to this unawareness. She paced the small length of her office, reading, perhaps aloud, her lips moving. I watched her, and a premonition formed: Abby doing likewise, while living with me.

At thirty, I was intrigued by synchronicity, and the possibility that it wasn't crap. My birthday dinner was set for Blue Sotto, until Rebecca realized she'd screwed up the reservation date. We had to search afresh and happened upon Akihiro after being turned away at Aquafire. The universe had therefore conspired to put Abby before me. Kismet? I was still loyal to human agency. I knew to take the next step, when I awoke at four a.m., wondering about her. Where was she from? What did she like to do? Was she good with her hands? I couldn't *not* return to her the following night. And now here she was, my inevitable wife, refilling my water cup, cooking me protein-rich meals, standing at the ready, all positivity and light. Had I taken my pills? When was my last bowel movement? Did I need anything? Yes. For her to go to work or a museum, anywhere but helicoptering over my life.

In June, I graduated from chair to crutches. Right crutch, left leg, left crutch, right leg, repeat. My robotic four-limbed march, hup-two-three-four. Concentrating on the steps of my hobbled, four-point gait was like learning a complicated new dance or listening to avant garde jazz, exhausting.

On our living room wall, Newman's *Onement VI* contrasts Abby's photographs. Two expansive panels of deep blue bisected by a single white line. The panel on the left appears slightly smaller than the one on the right, but that impression is a distortion caused by the gradations of blue. People misinterpret the white line as a rip in space-time or a division in the canvas. Instead, the line merges the panels. Ocean and sky. Day and night. The zip is the shared space between artist and viewer. Meaning arises from duality, just as a text requires a writer and a reader, a marriage requires a wife and a wife.

Binarisms deliver oneness. Abby had purchased the print for me the week we moved in together, a gesture toward opening space for me. On nights I returned beat from work and irritated by the colossal waste of time sitting in traffic or coercing recalcitrant programmers to finish their code, those panels of blue were my TV, my mandala, my sanctuary. My eyes traveled over them until the blues calmed me, but that was before. After an hour of physical therapy, which at that point had progressed to four days per week, I was spent. I lay on the couch, gazing at *Onement*, not feeling wholeness, only separation. The two disparate sides rifted my body until I sank into the couch and, not pacified, I fell sleep.

Despite my awkward, mechanical gait, and my unending battle with fatigue, I felt bolstered and newly independent, being free of the wheelchair. I could look at people at eye level again. And one night I wanted to feel freer and more like my old self.

"Abby."

"Yes?"

"I miss sex," I said.

"So do I."

Abby's touch over the last several months had been guarded, careful, like I was a burn victim, my skin too raw to withstand any pressure. I missed the uninhibited touch of seduction, the strong ownership of her knowing hands, not the obligatory light, absent-minded rub of the shoulders. "Can we try?" I asked.

"Should we?"

"Tricia said the pelvic floor muscles are like any other muscles in the body. Use them or lose them."

"And your sisters…"

"A dermatologist and podiatrist?"

"They're still doctors. They have a base level of universal knowledge, and they've had kids."

"Jenny removes moles and skin tags all day. She throws creams at psoriasis and burns off warts. And Paige does her own disgusting things with feet. Kids ruin the pelvic floor, but not like gunshot wounds, falling down stairs, and invasive surgeries that make a metal birdcage of your bones."

I had ruined the moment.

Abby and I, for the most part, had enjoyed a sustained and robust sex life in our marriage. Certainly, we'd endured periods of stress and amateur fumbling or inattention. We'd blown past the point of orgasm and then gotten too sensitive to continue. I'd make her come and then not want to be touched. Or she'd bring me to orgasm and I'd fall asleep. We'd left one another unsatisfied. We'd gone months without touching each other. We'd masturbated, mutual and alone. We'd perfected five-minute missionary. Our creativity and laughter, give and take, and full attention gave rise to everything from furious fucks to slower lovemaking. Candles and eye contact, dildos and clamps, two fingers, three. All of which came with the natural ebb and flow of mood and togetherness, of separation and longing, of knowing and ignorance, of closeness and distance in marriage.

A few days later I tried again. I began by kissing Abby's neck, her ear, her mouth. My left hand found its way between buttons, under a bra, to skin and nipple. My body flooded with memory and sensation, thrill and energy, and then hope, a sense of home, of lightness, but briefly, so briefly, because pain closely trailed and vanquished the small pleasure I felt. This sex, if we can call it that, was unlike any sex Abby and

I had had previously together, or with anyone else. We were cautious, so cautious, dealing with an aging, damaged canvas. Abby didn't want to hurt me. I didn't want to hurt. If I moved too fast or twisted in just the right way, I'd get a sear of pain in my lower abdomen or deep in my hip. When Abby tried to enter me, she couldn't. My vaginal muscles clamped and burned. I couldn't straddle her, nor roll around with her. On my back I couldn't hold my legs open comfortably or for very long. My hip ached. My back stung. Sharp jolts accompanied any quick movements of my pelvis. I hated girls who lay still, and here I was now one of them, stunned, unmoving, unhappy in my changed body, impotent and aching.

Abby went to the store during my next session with Tricia. "We tried to have sex."

"How did that go?"

I was lying on a massage table she'd left at the house for my treatments. She'd wrapped a belt around her waist and my right thigh. When she pressed her weight against the belt, stretching my hip, I felt a profound relief, as the cement in the joint turned into loose sand.

"It didn't. I was tighter than tight and it hurt."

"Penetration or everything?"

"Everything."

"It was too soon. Now we know. You're frustrated, but think of the experience as informational. Any new thing you try at this point tells us something useful. It helps me better help you. Was penetration painful at initial entry or deeper?"

"Initial. Couldn't go deeper. It was too painful to get that far."

"Are you having any incontinence?"

"What does that have to do with anything?"

She unbuckled the belt and started working on the railroad scar on my belly, pinching and rolling the thick bump and the tissue around it, pulling, cajoling the glued fibers. I hated this part. It made me think of my body as nonconforming dough.

"I'm just being thorough. It sounds like you're experiencing vaginismus, which is a fancy term for painful spasms of the vaginal muscles. Ever experienced it before?"

"Never."

"Here's the thing. In response to pain or trauma, the body wages the most efficient and intelligent response it knows, but muscles are dumb. They do two things. They quit and go on vacation, get inhibited, or they clamp down with all their might and spasm and protect."

"My vagina is protecting me from having sex with my wife? How's that intelligent? How is that possible? I've had a whole hand in me." Rebecca's hand, her left one, which was slightly smaller than her right. We had worked up to full entry, fucking frequently and furiously, playing at two fingers, three, until five were crammed pussy-deep to the third knuckles, then lubing and rocking and gingerly pushing, pushing, pushing until Rebecca's arm ended at her wrist. "I'm sorry. You probably don't want to hear about that. But, no, I'm not a bad faucet, not yet anyway. I don't leak."

"I don't mind," she said. "Takes more than that to shock me. I spend a lot of time with people. They tell me all kinds of things. I get better stories than a bartender. I worked on a seventy-year-old's neck for about three months so she could deep throat her husband again without being laid up with neck pain and a migraine for a week."

"You bill insurance for that?"

"Sex is an activity of daily living, a quality-of-life concern. My goal is always to get people back to doing whatever it is they want to be doing. Help them be their best selves physically so the rest can follow. It might interest you to know that there's a physiological reason the vagina allows itself to be fisted. It's called SAID, Specific Adaptation to Implied Demand."

"Use it or lose it."

"Yep."

"So I've lost it."

"For now, but it's not permanent. I can help with the physical—muscles, nerves, fascia, but the emotional, psychological, PTSD stuff is out of my scope of practice. You should talk to someone about that."

"About my too-tight pussy?"

"About underlying factors contributing to muscle tension and pain in the pelvic bowl."

I nodded, though we both knew I wouldn't talk to anyone. I wasn't even talking to myself at that point. Tricia continued to work on me, and my muscles stretched and gave. They *adapted to demand* little by little with all the poking, pressing, and extending. Through the treatment, and though Abby hadn't talked to him in months, I heard David's voice, asking, accusing Abby, "You're letting someone else massage your wife's vagina?" No. Because what Tricia did wasn't massage. Hers was a technical process. She knew right where to press, as if her touch were a magnet drawn to pain.

"This will go faster if you do some of the stretching on your own or have Abby help," she told me. "I'm happy to instruct the two of you."

"I don't want to make our life, especially our sex life, any more clinical than it already is."

At fifty-two, Abby looked fabulous. She had thwarted the twenty-pound estrogen belly that comes with a midlife shrug. She moved easily around the house, quietly floating, while I galumphed in the ponderous metal of my wheelchair, later, plodding along, foot, crutch, foot, crutch, with my sloppy, softening muscle tone. I longed for my body's previous efficiencies, its instinctual adaptations. Regaining the smallest bit of endurance took several months. Daily walks. Short and full of breaks at first. Breathless walks. Small laps in the house, couch to counter, counter to window, window to chair. Then five minutes outside, to the corner and back. Fifteen lines in the concrete, sixteen slabs. Don't step on a crack. The ground repelled and jarred me, but the fresh air and the chilled silence of June, almost summer, welcomed me. Wind and the nattering crows, the water, always the water near, almost dissolved the strong, untouchable ache in my pelvis. My abdomen, center of mass, torn open and scarred back together, made me walk like an unpracticed drunk. My trunk had thickened in marbled chunks along and under the incision line. *Scar tissue. Keep touching it. Massaging it. The adhesions will break up.* Sometimes Abby walked with me. Sometimes I went alone. I preferred the latter. I was slow, her constant vigilance annoyed and depressed me.

I had been grateful for Abby in the hospital, for her steady watchful eyes, her calming hand on my head, face, or arm. I had been grateful for her since turning thirty. Once home, however, more often than not, I wanted to be alone. I knew she felt helpless and was doing all she could to be a good wife and carry me through. I knew above all that she was on my side, but that knowledge didn't change my ornery need to be away from her.

"You should go back to work before you lose your job," I told Abby one afternoon when I was lying on the sofa after a physical therapy appointment. "We'll need the money."

"I still don't think you should be alone for long stretches."

"I'm fine. I'm walking with a cane now. My balance is getting better."

"You know what I mean," she said.

I did, but there was no reason to admit it. I was fighting depression, loss of self and place. "Separate time is necessary in relationships," I said, quoting her.

"You have to see people."

"Do I?" I said.

Abby was so good at leveling her responses, at not reacting to nuance or tone. "Your mom has asked to come out."

"It's not a good time," I said, though I was a family girl and I loved seeing my parents. After moving to Seattle, where they weren't an easy thirty minutes away, I had longed for them to visit. Twenty-three hundred miles was a trek, and holidays, once boisterous days of decadence and nonsense bickering, were a subdued trial with just Abby and me. Now, however, I craved solitude. I didn't want to have to rise out of myself to entertain or even be present for others. I'd lost my stunning personality along with my body.

Reluctantly, Abby obliged me by returning to work, two days a week, then four and finally five, occasionally working a sixth day. My guess was she found as much relief in the time away as I did. With the house to myself—myself to myself— I groped for what to do, and battled all indoctrination about being productive, doing *something*. The positivity of busy-ness was a hard notion to drop. My mind betrayed me with endless questions. My body with its pains and lack of endurance stymied all momentum. The physical world took on a hardness. Objects of comfort—the bed, the sofa, the heated seats of the car—morphed into obstacles. In any case, my body was immune to comfort, which stirred in philosophical arguments. Cartesian mind-body divisions versus Beauvoir's feminist embodiment. My stomach was no longer smooth and soft. My thighs, once rugby-strong, had atrophied and now bore long, mottled, misshapen scars that crisscrossed joggled skin and tissue. My face was offset. The flesh around my eye near the fractured cheekbone and orbit crinkled and pulled oddly, causing my eye to appear recessed and smaller than its mate. Each time I saw myself naked I thought of Picasso's women and I understood Frida Kahlo better. We are bodies in the world and understand the world through them, but my body had overwhelmed my capacity to understand. I was barraged with sensations, and all my mind could manage was resignation and the simple idea that there is nothing necessary about why the world is, or why the world is as it is.

On someone's advice—her psychiatrist, her mother?—the female shooter, the gungirl who survived, wrote individual letters of apology to the families of those killed and to the wounded survivors. My letter sat in a drawer, unopened. Sat past my immediate recovery, past months of silence, past the day the last reporters stood outside my door, past her trial and sentencing. She was found guilty of eleven counts of murder and was awarded eleven life sentences without parole.

I watched the ferries.

I stared at the divided panels of blue on our living room wall.

I watched the Seattle sky. Its panels of matte-gray clouds depleted the land and water of color. Everywhere I looked was muted by gray.

I was alone in grief, in reckoning. As a visitor to Rookwood, I'd been an outsider. I lived thirteen hundred miles away and couldn't attend community support groups or vigils. I couldn't leave flowers or stuffed animals, three dollar Mary candles, or other tokens of sorrow and remembrance. I was alone.

Then a package arrived.

A thick, large envelope.

From the gungirl, the culprit survivor.

A manila envelope, institution-stamped. An unopened elephant. I caged it in a drawer.

WILDERNESS

LIST OF TIPS FOR COPING:

1. KEEP THE PHONE NUMBER OF A GOOD FRIEND NEARBY.
2. ALLOW YOURSELF TO FEEL PAIN. IT WILL PASS.
3. TAKE CARE OF YOUR MIND AND BODY.
   A. REST, SLEEP, AND EAT HEALTHY MEALS.
   B. EXERCISE, THOUGH NOT TO EXCESS.
   C. MEDITATE.
4. RECALL WHAT HELPED YOU COPE IN THE PAST.
   THINK ABOUT WHAT GIVES YOU HOPE NOW.
   LEAN ON BOTH.

Vague rules. Nothing in my history touched what I needed in order to cope now. Near the list, the crime victim's hotline. Reminders all around about how I'm supposed to survive, to persevere, to deal, to transcend, but I don't want to say a fucking word or do a fucking thing, so I walk. Long hours. I walk myself into a fatigued limp. I try to walk correctly, but my body won't obey. I've lost muscle mass, power, strength, endurance, balance, control. *The femoral nerve activates the quad muscles. Yours has been damaged, thus the atrophy. The functional unit of a muscle is a sarcomere. You've lost sarcomere length, girth, and numbers.* The walking initially had specific purposes—to improve my endurance and strength, to get me outside. Walking signified recovery and normalcy. Despite the ache, I kept walking, making it my new routine. *Use it or lose it. The body adapts.* And then walking became a compulsion, as if I could walk out of my mind. I walked longer distances, and for no reason that I could discern I always walked north, past the ferry dock and along the water at Lincoln Park, slowly through the crowding neighborhoods, with cars lining the curbs before modern box houses with rooftop views worth a million dollars. This was once a spacious part of the city, a quiet get-away from the stadiums and tourists. Now people infested everywhere, and the squeeze is getting worse. Acutely aware of other people's avidity, I stand back from it. I skirt sidewalks and walk in the street or on the grass to avoid interaction. I always wear sunglasses. I'm sure I'm mistaken by neighbors and shopkeepers for a reserved or aloof bitch. Distance, though, does not equate to disdain. Distance is protective and permissive. Distance keeps me anonymous. Distance allows me not to engage.

I walk the rain-heavy, concrete sidewalks. Pedestrians speckle my route. Car horns and mufflers blast the daylight hours. Bike tires on glistening streets make a sound like tearing silk. Otherwise silence rules beneath gray skies. Tufts of grass sprout from cracks, wilderness and organic matter trying to emerge, trying to combat development. I continue along Alki, under the bridge and toward the water side of the stadiums where the earth has been disturbed by a giant, tunneling drill. I pass the wastelands of demolition and construction into Pioneer Square with its aging red warehouses, ivy glomming the brick. And pigeons, pigeons. And men and kids, gutter punks, a few women. Pleas for spare change echo around me until I hobble through them toward a bench. The pigeons reluctantly yield their turf as I slowly pass. My pelvis and right leg throb, as I collapse on the wooden seat. I've walked an impossible ten miles over almost five hours. After several minutes the throbbing dies into a dull pulse and low ache. Abby and I had the Great Wall for our next vacation, or possibly the El Camino. My pelvis vetoed both. My pelvis told me that though I had not died, other things had—dreams and an imagined future. Vacations that involved walking. The future would be filled with constant adjustments. I sat on the bench and tried not to move.

"What you got going on?" a man asked. "The gout got you? I saw you limping." He stood before me in dirty khakis and an oversized Seahawks sweatshirt. He kept his eyes downcast and shuffle-hopped between his two feet like he had to run off to pee.

"Something like that."

"Gout's nasty. Gets your toe all fat and hot and hard to walk on. Doc says it's crystals in the joint, but crystals, shit, you can't tell the future from my toe." He pulled his left foot from its boot. His sock had developed a hole around his first toe. He wiggled his toes. "See? There ain't no future."

"You're right about that," I said. "The present is all we have. No guarantees."

The man tucked his hoof back into his boot. He frowned. "You don't make no sense."

"Not a lot does."

"What's that you say?"

"Life is nasty, brutish, and short."

He frowned. More lines appeared on his face. He dismissed me with a hard wave across his body and lumbered to a nearby trashcan. "No sense," he muttered. "Nonsense." He rooted around, consigning me to oblivion.

The spontaneity, the randomness, the unjustifiability of the world wouldn't leave me. There is nothing pre-ordained about men with gout or pigeons, nor about America or glaciers, or the fact of gravity. There is nothing inevitable about humans or human nature or the earth revolving around the sun. The universe could have been made to operate in countless ways. No creator, of course. Not necessary. We're stuck, without explanation, with the way the earth spins, forever unable to know the essence of anything. Abby went to therapy on and off until she was twenty-five. "I was reading a book called *The Denial of Death*. I assumed the therapist would know it because the book was famous in psychology circles, but she didn't. That was a let-down. I explained the thesis, that everything we do, we do only to allay a deep fear of death, refusing to admit that we're going to die, basically lying to ourselves about ourselves all the time. 'That's a bleak view of our motives.' That was her verdict. But I knew it to be true, bleak or not. She wouldn't engage with me about it at all. Thing is, I don't think the idea is bleak. We just happen to be here and we *are* going to die. That gives us reason to live more consciously."

We're the lucky ones, lucky us.

I felt my own face, pensive and straining. I sat in a deep fatigue on the bench. Beyond the pigeons in the square lay uninspired art galleries. Past those, several piers, and past the piers, farther out, Pike Place Market with its flurried tourists bumping backs and elbows, shuffling along the concrete floors, funneling past the vendors and their wares. It was probably due to Abby that I never saw the draw of the market. Crowded. Dirty. Too many smells, some pleasant, most not. Aloof artists pretending not to be salesmen. Visitors traipse through by the millions. Yes, the market is old and, yes, it's fun to watch a fish get thrown around, but there's no reason to see it twice. Past the market, further north is Olympic Sculpture Park. I had hoped to reach the park and play peekaboo with the statues hidden in the tall grass. The park, which sits atop sixty years of soil and ground water contamination, contains Louise Nevelson's *Sky Landscape I*. In painted aluminum, two totems reach toward the sky, but not in straight trajectories, rather in deformations of metal and space, never touching. Some days, one of the totems appears to kneel before the other, but they both might as easily look like they're dancing. Though metal, the piece floats and moves. I looked at pictures of Nevelson's boxes in a high school art class. Wooden objects of urban detritus couched in small, intimate settings, as if you'd opened someone's secret drawer.

By Pioneer Square, I was leaden in my own body, unable to move. I was spent. I sat on a bench. Hours later, I bussed home. Abby had returned to work, and I was glad to have the house to myself. I collapsed on the couch. Outside, the rain continued. Trees held their stations, bowing slightly. With the rain arrived an overwhelming sense of stillness. Seattle rain, while relentless, was not angry, not full of erratic wind, lightning or thunder. The couch welcomed me. Finally I slept.

At first I didn't want any news, names, or numbers. Details. None of it. I didn't want to know that there were three perpetrators, one who survived, a girl who wasn't fast enough in turning the gun on herself. A sniper nipped her in the shoulder before she could complete her part of the plan. Forty-two, thirty-one. Retired jersey numbers. A hundred others on the premises left with their individual scars. A town rocked by insult. Prayers and flowers flooding in as if they could appease a lion's roar.

Then I shifted. I let the information in all at once. Data. Which was all it was and data is what I knew, what I was fluent in. The currency of my daily transactions. Zeros and ones. That's how I processed the onslaught pouring in about that day.

Robert, Jacob, Amanda.

Seventeen, seventeen, seventeen.

12:42pm. Fourth period.

Data points. Strings of code.

I plumbed archives. The first school shooting occurred in 1764, before the U.S. was even the U.S. Then from 1764 to 1964, deaths and injuries arrived in zeros and ones and twos. A mass shooting requires four or more deaths, excluding that of the perpetrators, who are mostly white males. On corkboard in the office, I posted the years and the schools and the numbers:

1966 UNIVERSITY OF TEXAS 17 DEAD 31 INJURED

1998 THURSTON 4 DEAD 25 INJURED

1998 WESTSIDE MIDDLE 5 DEAD 10 INJURED

1999 COLUMBINE 13 DEAD 23 INJURED

2005 RED LAKE 9 DEAD 5 INJURED

2007 VIRGINIA TECH 32 DEAD 23 INJURED

2012 NEWTOWN 26 DEAD 2 INJURED

2014 PILCHUCK 4 DEAD 2 INJURED

2015 UMPQUA CC 9 AND 9

2016 ROOKWOOD 42, 31

The list was incomplete. A beginning. I could add and subdivide, categorize farther. Mass shootings. School shootings. Gang shootings. Competitive shooting. Others. More. Mass as multiple. Massacre—result of a spree, an event with no cooling-off period. Unrest. It made me sad to think how much carnage I failed to notice and record, not that schools were unique. Consider Orlando, June 2016. Forty-nine dead at a nightclub. Safety is a grand delusion.

"This can't be healthy," Abby said as she looked over the corkboard.

Then on a different day, she asked, "What are you getting out of this? There's no understanding these events. They're nonsensical and unforgivable."

"Psychopath. Is that the right term?" Abby said when she saw the letters.

Still, later, "Why not get involved with lobbying for gun control, if you want to do something constructive? I know," she said. "Too much money behind it all."

"How can you bear all this research? And the gungirl? You can't save her. She can't save you. Liz? Are you listening?"

Data points. I chased their logic. The safety of patterns. Abby couldn't see what I saw. She couldn't understand zeros and ones. She couldn't see me. Circling back to Rookwood,

I found I was part of the worst mass school shooting to date, and one of few involving a female.

LIST OF TIPS FOR COPING:

1. RE-ESTABLISH NORMAL ROUTINES ASAP.
2. MAKE SMALL DECISIONS DAILY. THIS WILL BRING BACK A FEELING OF CONTROL.
3. KEEP A JOURNAL AND WRITE YOUR FEELINGS AND THOUGHTS DOWN TO RELEASE THEM.
4. UNDERTAKE TASKS WITH CARE. ACCIDENTS ARE MORE LIKELY TO HAPPEN AFTER SEVERE STRESS.
5. TAKE UP PAINTING, POTTERY, OR SCULPTURE. ALL ARE CATHARTIC.

The ferries traveled their routes. Sometimes restlessness took me, and if I saw another boat, I felt a sinking inside. I'd have to get away from the house and the water. I lengthened my walks. In skate parks all over the city boys of all ages shredded in skinny black jeans or cargo shorts, plain T-shirts and scabbed elbows. On every corner, a coffee stand. I walked even longer, later in the day, walked into the deep ache of my pelvis, through downtown and east into the Capitol Hill neighborhood. I stopped in bars, drawn by chatter emerging through door cracks. I threw back a shot and moved on, overwhelmed by the cacophony and young faces. On Capitol Hill, coffee shops, bars, toy stores, tattoo parlors, and piercing studios vied for space, lining the streets. Through plate glass I watched artists and bodies.

I heard the *zzzzzzzzzzz* of needles. I watched puckered nipples get pierced by stainless steel pins. I saw faces writhing.

I'd thumbed portfolios, and returned to Indigo Blues to admire the cool, concentrated reserve of the tattooists, their detached professionalism. Inking, like piercing, is an intimate art. I could see the attraction to adorning the skin, the fun in piercing someone's labia or nipple. All a succession of intimacies with strangers.

A woman stopped beside me to watch. "Thinking of getting some ink?" she asked.

"I don't know. I've never been into tattoos all that much."

"It's mesmerizing, the process."

"Definitely has its appeal."

"I'm Alice." She stretched a tattooed sleeve toward me to shake hands. "I've seen you before. I work here. Let me know if you want a closer look."

"Liz. Yeah, thanks."

"Forgive me for saying so, but you seem like you've been through something."

"You could say that."

"Need to commemorate it?"

I was not one to wear misery as a badge. I disdained pity and those who solicited it. I suppose my penchant for privacy was a Midwestern carryover. I thought about what sort of tattoo could possibly mark me in ways I wasn't already marked. A bull's eye? A number? I could go with a clichéd quote about what doesn't kill me.

Alice said, "Tattoos are as old as we are. They trace all the way back to Otzi, the Iceman. There are loads of reasons to get one, tribal, healing, punishment, spiritual, decorative. You name it, I'll do it, but no tears or swastikas. Oh, and no Care Bears. And no Smurfs. No Disney, either. I guess I have more rules than I realized." She disappeared back into the buzz, and

I carried on down Broadway into Volunteer Park. The museum and conservatory were long closed, and the park was empty except for the late-night yoga. I assumed it was a diversion for the clean and sober who needed a Tuesday-night activity that didn't involve a smoky bar or aerosol huffs in a basement. I stood to the side, trying to hide behind a tree. I mimicked their movements as best I could, but my body wouldn't bend and curl and twist. Yoga was supposed to be restorative but I quickly grew irritated again with my limitations. When we first moved to Seattle, Abby and I got interested in yoga. My body moved freely back then, and the classes we took led us to the Kama Sutra. For a few weeks, instead of yoga in the park, we practiced yoga in bed. The pleasant memory soured my mood even more. I gave up on plow pose while the group broke their necks with crane. I sat on a picnic table, embedded in self-pity.

An hour later I walked past Indigo Blues again. Alice stood outside vaping. She sucked in. The end of her pen flared blue and faded, flared and faded.

"I didn't take you for a smoker," I said.

"Marijuana," she said, offering me a hit. I still wasn't used to weed being legal, its use in public, its musty scent in unexpected places.

I took the pen. "How does this thing work?"

"Stick your lips there and suck it. Breathe in like a joint. The cannabis heats in that canister to four hundred degrees. THC breaks free into vapor. Supposedly, it's better for the lungs than smoking and easier to dose than edibles, not to mention all the sugar and garbage that goes into cookies. I keep trying to convince the store owners to run a line of dairy-free, gluten-free, sugar-free pot whatevers. Moneymaker, I tell ya. Now, about your tattoo."

"Still on the fence."

"For you, I sense the therapeutic angle. Women come in here a lot after mastectomies to make art out of their scars or get a tattoo after some other loss. Ownership and control of the trauma and all that."

"The false sense of it."

"Doesn't feel that way to them."

"They're fooling themselves."

"Placebo effect is still an effect."

"I almost died not too long ago," I said, despite myself.

"Proclaim your survival."

Inside, Alice cleaned and prepped a table and aligned her ink capsules on a bench. With a warm towel and some disinfectant, she cleaned her canvas—the skin on the back of my shoulder. She leaned into me, needle to the blade, blazing deep, thick, confident lines. She pulled the canvas taut, placing, replacing her hand at will, as needed, grasping the flesh, making, creating. I felt not quite molested but encroached on. A sexual, animal act, this strange woman called Alice crawling over my surface, owning me. The energy of creativity. A more inhibited person would have felt violated. With Alice, so close that I could feel her breath, kneading and marking my tissues, I grew warm inside. I wanted ink all over my body, wanted the tattoo hour to last longer.

"Come back when you're ready for more," she said. "Watching is one thing. Doing is another."

TODAY'S TIP, PAMPHLET NOISE:

BEING SHOT BY A GUN IS TRAUMATIC. YOU MAY FEEL SHOCK. YOU MAY FEAR FOR YOUR SAFETY. YOU MAY FEEL DEPRESSED

OR ANGRY, BOTH OF WHICH ARE NORMAL FOR SOMEONE WHO HAS GONE THROUGH THIS TYPE OF PHYSICAL VIOLATION. THESE FEELINGS ARE NOT SIGNS OF WEAKNESS. THEY SHOULD BE HONORED. YOU MAY NOTICE OTHER SYMPTOMS, TOO, SUCH AS ANXIETY, REPETITIVE REHASHING OF THE EVENT, NIGHT-MARES OR TROUBLED SLEEP, IRRITABILITY OR IRRATIONAL BEHAVIORS, SADNESS, LOW ENERGY. CARE FOR YOURSELF AND HEAL EMOTIONALLY AS WELL AS PHYSICALLY. IF YOU FEEL OVERWHELMED BY THESE FEELINGS, OR IF THEY LAST MORE THAN THREE WEEKS, CONTACT YOUR DOCTOR. THERE ARE TREATMENTS THAT CAN HELP YOU.

I wasn't shot by a gun. I was shot by a PERSON with a gun. A human being. A teenager. A girl. Three weeks? Fuck you. Prozac? Fuck you, too.

The ferries shuttled through Thanksgiving, Christmas, New Year's, my fortieth birthday.

In the past, I had always made something of my birthday. Age five: Chuck E. Cheese. Ten: roller rink. Sixteen delivered a mariachi band to serenade me. Two years later I threw a Skid Row Eighteen-and-Life prison party. New York City welcomed me at twenty-one. Thirty: Akihiro. Birthdays to me were a big deal. Genetics and the miraculous had conspired to produce me, and I had triumphed over death for another year. At forty, I sat alone thinking, *Why me? Why now? What the fuck?*

I grew more restless.

I'd never purposefully shunned Abby. I always had some-thing to tell her. I always *wanted* to tell her things, mundane and not. I loved how she stopped whatever she was doing and trained her whole body toward me. She seemed never to tire of my long-windedness. Now I'd tired of talking to her.

They say depression is anger turned inward. A long, severe recession. More than sadness. A flaw in chemistry, perhaps.

The girl, the teenager with a gun. I read what she'd sent. She is clearly highly intelligent and traumatized. Considering what she's gone through, I almost feel sympathy for her. Almost. It's hard to hold conflicting emotions, to sit belly-deep in the gray, but in Seattle, gray prevails.

TIP FOR COPING: REVERT TO WHAT YOU KNOW.

Collar/Bar had two levels. The upstairs held a bar and dance floor that looked like any other, except for an eight-by-eight glass floor that revealed the space below. I paid ten dollars for a demo and tour. Underground, accessed by membership only, hosted a medieval arena of spectacle, stretching labyrinthine into rooms and passageways. Long chains dropped from the ceiling, where suspension points bolted into large beams filigreed the room. A beautiful circular wooden platform swayed from thick chains amid an array of medical exam tables. Along one wall four St. Andrew's crosses stood waiting, a fifth was occupied. A wooden platform swung empty. On the lower level talking and social discussion were banned. Only those at play could speak. During a demo, moderators spoke and allowed questions. A demo happened to be underway, and the tour paused before the flogging at the fifth cross. Naked and bound to the thick-beams of the wooden x: Rebecca. We stared at each other. For every second she didn't return her eyes to her master's feet she got flogged harder, yet she grinned and grinned and kept looking at me.

After the demo and tour ended, Rebecca found me upstairs. She embraced me, and I felt my body wilt into hers.

"How are you here?" I asked.

"In a way, I never left. You know me, I lose myself. Came to see you in the hospital, and, well, I stuck around town for the week, met this woman. We're playing tag. She comes to San Fran. I come here."

"You live in San Francisco now?"

"I should have moved there years ago. You'd be surprised where life has taken me."

"And Rachel?"

Rebecca shook her head.

"How long?"

"She overdosed five years ago."

I fumbled to give belated condolences, but Rebecca waved me off. She'd enjoyed or maybe not enjoyed their time together, but that life was over. Rebecca was immersed in the next experience, filled with purpose and sobriety.

"You're better?" she asked. "You're good?"

I didn't respond, too distracted by the tight leather contraption she was wearing. It looked like one long strap made to pull down across her nipples, crossing between her legs and up her backside. D-rings and clamps held it on place. "What *is* all this?"

Rebecca grinned the grin that made most people want to slap her. "You might not like what I'm into. In fact, I'm surprised you're here. Why are you here?"

She was right to be surprised. Collar/Bar was not my scene, nor had I ever even feigned interest in anything kinkier than self-release handcuffs or light anal play. I'd never dreamed of being hog-tied or peed on or probed like a medical specimen.

I didn't want to be hoisted to the ceiling and plugged like a socket. I preferred mutual lust, two bodies meeting in equal amounts of strength and control, give and take.

"Just wandering around."

"I have to go," she said. "I'm floor monitor tonight." She didn't move. She studied my eyes for some seconds. I was more than a little drunk, and she was not drunk at all. Who leaned toward whom is impossible to know, but Rebecca's hands held my face and brought my lips toward hers. I'd forgotten her strong kiss, her demanding tongue. After a few seconds more, she pulled back and looked at me again. I felt I hadn't been recognized in some time. "Come to this address later, around two," she said, handing me an address card not much bigger than a quarter. "I bet you'd appreciate some control these days." Then she touched a fob to an employee door and disappeared.

I sat in the bar and drank another whiskey and coke. I watched social exchanges and wondered how strangers came so quickly to an agreement of desires and followed each other downstairs. I'd read my share hook-up ads, for amusement of course. They sometimes made me think, albeit briefly, that going along with what other people want could be easy. Poly, kinky, curvy, married duo looking for another to be hot with. Adventurous, athletic, slutty MILF desirous of fun kink and someone who knows how to properly handle a woman. I could be those people—temporarily. But doing so would lead to too much talking, negotiating, hemming. Too much effort to coax the underlying need from the half-baked fantasy. Better to take a lesson from Collar/Bar.

From the barstool I watched silent agreements take place and co-conspirators disappear downstairs. I was an outsider and couldn't decode the signals. Barstools are lonely places to I escaped to the glistening streets. At two, I punched the numbers from the card into a keypad on an imposing, fifteen-story building.

"The owner travels for work," Rebecca said. "A group of us take turns hosting. I talked my way into the lineup a few weeks ago. The place is ours tonight."

The open space was not unlike the lower level of Collar/Bar, ornamented with beams and ropes and chains, cuffs of all kinds, flogs. Ropes and stays and metal braces. Apparatuses of increasing size.

"You get off on this?" I asked.

"Do I orgasm? Sometimes, yes. Most times I hum in euphoria. This sudden blend of head-high and body-high. It's hard to describe. I've acclimated to this over the last four years. Before that, I was just dabbling. I wasn't ready to commit." Rebecca slipped her thighs, ankles, and wrists into six points of standing restraints. "It *is* about sex and control but mainly about trust. I trust you, Liz, to help me reach the high I'm after. Do you trust yourself?" She handed me the stays and nodded toward a nearby table. On it were implements of all sizes and moods. "Go ahead," she said. "Destroy me."

After that, she did not speak, not even her safe word.

On the bus home, my body shook uncontrollably, expelling months of stored emotion. My arms ached and red rope burns had formed on my hands and wrists from pulling Rebecca's restraints. The bus was empty and dimly lit. I was grateful for the haze but rested my head in my hands just the same. I stayed home for the next three nights, watching over Abby's yard. The back fence had all but disappeared beneath some sort of green ivy. The stone garden lay empty and still, its three giant rocks like smooth, solitary islands. Abby had gone to Ohio. Her aunt, her last remaining family connection, had died.

Abby, my bride. What, if anything, was I going to tell her? How could I begin?

I was a thinking person, but I couldn't explain what I had done or why. In the backyard I stepped into the garden. The gravel dug into my bare feet. I went to the largest stone and sat down. The garden did not wash me in peace. My hip ached and my wrists felt strangled and weak. In my core—an unraveling. All the suturing the doctors had done, had taken such care with, was for naught. Rationally, I knew Abby's strength should have been my refuge, but Rookwood had submerged me in chaos. What I'd done with Rebecca did not classify as an affair. Affairs were frivolous. Affairs were for the weak. What I'd done did not feel frivolous. What I'd done felt necessary.

On Friday, I walked down Beach Drive, along Alki into SoDo, past the stadiums, and into Capitol Hill as I'd done before. I pressed the keypad and was soon buzzed in. I took the elevator to the sixth floor as I'd done before. Rebecca was inside, waiting. She had a robe on. Her muscular thighs tensed at me as she approached. The interior lights were off, but city light shone through the large windows that made up the west wall. The ferris wheel, still lit brightly, circled endlessly. The Space Needle, too, fired the sky. Implements were precisely organized around the room and symmetrically on a table.

Rebecca said, "I want you to take everything away."

"Have you been reading Beckett again?" I asked. I wasn't familiar with her forthright tone. I was used to the endless discussion and hypotheticals she'd dispensed at twenty. At forty, she spoke with economy and precision. "Why not a sensory deprivation tank? They're popular again," I said. I was nervous. I'd found my inexplicable way back to her, and I wasn't sure if I should linger.

"Tanks don't work for me. Someone else has to take everything away."

"Everything?"

"Everything."

Tricia had told me about a memoir by a man with Locked-In Syndrome. A Frenchman who'd had a stroke, which destroyed a specific part of his brainstem. He was aware, cognitively intact, but he couldn't move or speak. He could feel everything. His sense of touch was intact. He would itch but couldn't scratch. He could feel pain, but could do nothing to assuage it. The only way he could communicate was by blinking. Imagine the tortuously slow conversation. He'd had no choice. And now Rebecca claimed to seek the same austerity, albeit temporary. She said she wanted purity. She wanted to be blind, deaf, mute, tasteless, smell-less. To be rid of filters, devoid of disturbances. A mind un-corroded. We can be hard of hearing. We can lose or not have vision. There are those with no sense of smell, but we can't shut off our skins. Touch-blindness doesn't exist. Even burn victims generally retain some sensation.

"Why would you fuck with yourself like this? Our senses are necessary. They're how we know. The base of all knowledge."

"Why *wouldn't* you fuck with them? Our senses are the beginning of knowledge, but the mind has to interpret and make the final judgment. It's all perception," Rebecca said. "We have receptors all over the body that feed information to the brain. The brain is responsible for interpretation, for meaning. I'm not convinced that we can't reach a different level of knowledge. Change the input, change the knowledge, change the experience."

How do you speak a safe word if you're fully gagged?

How do you make a safe gesture if you're fully bound?

How do you blink to communicate if your eyes are covered?

We do unspeakable things to one another.

We do unspeakable things to ourselves.

Unspeakable, unseeable, unhearable, untasteable.

This is not sex.

This is beyond.

This is not transgression.

This is art.

"Why don't you just become someone's dog?" I asked.

"That's not interesting to me. I don't want to regress to an animal self. I want to transcend."

"Furiously shapeless," she said.

"Equal pressure everywhere on the skin," she said.

"I can do the same for you," she said.

I carry reasons. I can justify. Trauma. Stress reaction. Fight or flight. My body obeying basic autonomic physiological responses. My body willing my mind to surrender. My body searching for greater or lesser stimulus. My whole self searching for change.

My actions justified.

Given what I've been through, I get a pass.

A punch card.

I'm allowed to do unspeakable things.

For a while.

Right?
In this room, forever consensual.
In this room, a body, a nesting doll.
Everything inside, enclosed in successive wooden shells, painted, layered neatly over infinite dark hollows.

TONIGHT'S LIST OF TIPS FOR COPING:

1. PLACE PLUGS IN HER EARS.

2. PLACE A BALL IN HER MOUTH.

3. PLACE COTTON IN HER NOSTRILS.

4. PLACE TWO OPAQUE DISKS OVER HER EYES.

5. DON'T FORGET THE PLUGS FOR VAGINA AND ANUS.

6. SLOWLY WRAP HER BODY IN BLACK CLOTH.

7. WAIT.

LET IN THE RAIN-HEAVY AIR

I've sent apology letters to survivors. I guess I wanted to explain or something. Probably you don't care and don't want to hear any sort of explanation. Most of the letters have come back unopened. Basically they say, 'I'm sorry. Please carry on your life.' As if people need <u>my</u> permission to carry on. I'm nobody. But I wonder, is opening my letter a gesture of holding or moving? You tell me. I was surprised you wrote back. Some others did, but their letters were full of hate and I hope you die bitch and rot in hell bitch. Sometimes I think this whole thing is over and that everyone has forgotten me or is ignoring me. As they should. Banishment is the worst form of torture in many cultures. Then a hate letter arrives. They let me read everything that comes in. They think I should get what I deserve. But the powers above open everything first.

I've created a GIANT INTERRUPTION in your life. Your words. That's all it's been? That's not what the boys were after. Fuck shit up. Fuck shit UP. Fuck SHIT up. FUCKITALLUP. That's what they were after. Crazy destruction. Massive disintegration. Not an interruption. A pause. They would be so disappointed. Robbie scratched FUCKITALLUP into his shin. Just as the scab started to heal he'd grab a paper clip and etch the letters all over again, never letting the oozing and bleeding end. He would scrape and etch and push and drag repeatedly. It was mesmerizing.

It was gross. You know, we were ten when Columbine happened one-hundred fifty-six miles away.

> *Robert Henry Warden, 1999-2016.*
> *Jacob Dash Johnston, ibid.*
> *Amanda Jane Roberts, 1998—still alive.*
> *Fucking shit up.*

The boys would yell that at each other from fifty feet away then sprint and crash into each other. Muskox. Beasts. The smelled just as bad. The winner was the one who wasn't knocked out. They were insane. There wasn't a thing they wouldn't do. Fucking nutters as they say in England. Not boyish trucks and guns and snow machines. Not snowboard tricks and skateboard stunts. Jackasses plain and simple. Jackasses and worse. You know the types of guys to roll over and light their farts on fire? These were not those guys. These guys lit firecrackers in their underwear. They dropped stones off overpasses. They trapped and shaved squirrels. Robbie and Dash, fucking shit up at last. They broke quietly into people's homes at night. They didn't steal, not much anyway. They moved things around like ghosts would. There wasn't a thing they wouldn't do. I loved them. I thought I did. I'm supposed to figure that out. THEY want me to. There are two shrinks that tag-team me, Shrinky Dick and Lady Shrink. It's a race. Who will bond with me first and get the WHY OF EVERYTHING?

> *Inside my mind*
> *Everyone wants*
> *Inside my mind*

So the boys, yeah. I'm supposed to figure that out, my connection to them. How it started. Why I went along. Why I went wrong. I knew everything we did was wrong. Every thought. Every action. Wrong. Wrong. Wrong.

We were all freshman in detention together. I had gotten in trouble for smoking on school grounds. Robbie told a teacher to suck his dick and Dash had punched a kid in the nuts. That was week one of high school. We were all off to a grand start. We weren't friends yet, but we'd all taken note of each other.

Dash set up a row of bottle rockets under the bleachers at the homecoming game, but he'd forgotten fire. He saw me and asked for my lighter, lit everything, and, running past me, grabbing my arm, said, 'Run, whore! dragging me with him. We ran into the locker room where Robbie was setting off M80s. At an abandoned house I knew, we got stoned and graffiti'd the walls until two in the morning. They were friends because they liked fire and loud shit and both had tried to make pipe bombs. I always had weed and pills so they kept me around. Isn't it obvious why I went along with them? They made that stupid town interesting.

Today, Lady Shrink told me:

> It's simple, really. You think you can detach, but you can't. Other people do affect you.

Fuck other people. Other people are complete disappointments.

My room is cold. The white walls burn my eyes. Most days I have a headache. No one gets a roommate in here. Everyone gets a bed, a sink, a toilet, a small rectangle of natural light. I'm told every window has three layers of Plexiglas so there's no point trying to break it. The boys would have found a way. I think of them and I still do stupid things, as if they're watching me, waiting, wondering why I'm not with them.

Dash shaved our cat. He used to live in Florida with his mom, but she sent him to his dad because she couldn't deal with him anymore. He kept feeding mice to snakes he'd trapped and then he'd kill the snakes and leave them around the apartment complex for people to find. There was something about the neighbor's dog making a mess of the yard and lots of bones from different things. I was stoned when he told the story so I don't really remember. But he said he was going to join the Marines and was just preparing himself for the things he'd have to do as an undercover operative. The cat disappeared, probably because it was traumatized. My brother loved the stupid fucker. The cat was a stray who took to Todd immediately. The thing practically slept on his face at night. It would get all curled up on his pillow. I don't think Dash killed Todd's cat, but I can't be sure. There wasn't a thing Dash wouldn't do, but mostly he stayed in the basement and played SUPER COLUMBINE MASSACRE and HATRED. I hated those games and the bright, huge screen that burned my eyes.

Dash hurt things and Robbie hurt himself. He played this game where he'd lay down by the curb and cover himself with trash. He'd be there for hours sometimes, waiting for a car to roll over him. Finally, bored, he'd get up or he'd get up maybe because something in him promised something better would come along. I don't know what. He'd see how hard he could throw the back of his hand against a tree. Or he'd make bike ramps with steep slopes and ride backflips off them. He landed on his ass a lot. Sometimes they'd huff whippets before they ran at each other. Or he'd tell me to kick him in the nuts. He would try so hard not to flinch, but he always flinched *and usually fell to the ground. Robbie used to like to trace the scars on my skin and then pinch them and pick them. He wasn't gentle.*

All up and down my arms are cuts. On the back of my hands. My calves. My inner thighs. Thin red lines. White, raised scars. Straight and jagged marks, dots and long tendrils, crossing, interrupting. Tribal, but for variation in size, shape, the randomness of the cuts. I've been doing this, wrecking my skin. For a long time. On my shoulders. My belly. Breasts. Neck. I trace the embossed lines of my skin. The first time was an accident. I was in the kitchen putting dishes away. My dad was at the door, arguing with my step-mom. I don't know what about. It was always something. They were always fighting. I was looking toward the screen door and reaching for the silverware. I grabbed a steak knife, gashed my palm. Hurt like a motherfucker, but there was this rush and I lost my breath and then all of a sudden I was warm and calm and I couldn't hear the yelling. Like I'd gone deaf. Finally. Blissfully, utterly deaf. So I took a little knife from the drawer, a paring knife I guess they're called, for apples or pears, or a young girl's inner thighs, and kept it in my room.

In here they won't leave me alone with nail clippers. I can't shave my legs. I use plastic forks and knives. Even when I eat, someone watches. Someone is always watching. Almost always. I stole some binders from Shrinky Dick's office and unbelievably no one saw. In the binder, there's all this shit that's meticulously typed and annotated, little stickies on various pages, all color-coordinated. He calls himself organized, that dude, a control enthusiast. He tells me his wife used to find his quirks endearing. Used to. They're having some trouble staying attuned*. His word. He tells me personal things because he thinks I give a shit.*

The binder has loads to drop. Heavy stinking loads:

> She has taken those first acts of self-mutilation and
> embedded them into a larger mythology. Cutting
> is no longer simple. Cutting is more than a red gash
> acting as a temporary salve to a deep psychological
> wound. A scar, a memory, a chronological marker
> of repeated insult to the self, by oneself and by others.
> The red and white lines are bound in a larger distortion
> of attempting to create meaning for oneself. Trying to
> make pain more than pain. Trying to make pain and
> its visual aftermath an art. Writing pain on the body
> for anyone willing to look, to see. She wears her scars
> on the skin. Through the looking there may be a
> chance of healing or salvation.

*Shrinky Dick Dude is lofty in his thinking, elevating my simple
act of destruction and release to religious salvation. Sorry Dicky
Dude, no one gets saved. No one's saving anyone.*

> Sociology is loaded with examples of bloody rites
> of initiation into adulthood—removing a tooth;
> cutting a chunk from an earlobe; tattooing or
> scarifying the face, arms, back, breast; excising the
> clitoris or foreskin. These serve as permanent records,
> clear divisions, between past and future, male and
> female. They denote membership into a community,
> the end of childhood and beginning of adulthood.
> Cutters belong to a community of one. They cut alone.
> They cut often. They cut over past cuts. There is no
> clear division between then and now, young or old.

Everything is now.

*I think the dude's going to write a book about me. And why not?
Someone should get rich off the shit I did. Or maybe you will, keeper
of the diary dribble. Drivel. Vocab word of the day. The shrinks
and staff still make me do school here. Court orders. Finish the
GED. For what? Oh, yeah, so I can sound smart in letters and
interviews. So I can be a literate inmate. For life.*

*Feel the August heat carry into September. Vicious, viscous heat,
suffocating as it fills a gymnasium crowded with slouching, sweating teenagers hip to hip, holding elbows in, breathing shallowly,
avoiding contact. Their teachers are watching, waiting, helpless.
They, too, breathe slowly, shallowly. They try to understand. They
try to see. But they can't. Few could. The damp heat can't be
blamed. The damp heat obscures nothing. It can only be felt.*

*They're slouching, their heads bowed, all heads, teachers' too, all
shoulders, bowed, slumped. Silence, a new silence. The halls for
weeks will allow only harsh, soft whispers. Did you know? Would
you? Who cares? Why did it happen? Why did they do this, exactly? Why? They will be careful. They will walk gingerly on the
tiled floors. They will eye each other without seeing. They will try
to see. They will think things they never thought. They will see
death as a possibility, love too—if they allow themselves to call it
that, dangerous as it is. They will know for an instant that they
are not immortal, that no one is, but that their actions can be.
When weeks have passed, they will go on like we all go on. They
will forget for long periods then suddenly remember. And forget
again. And remember. Their whole lives will be marked by this
primary tragedy, but also other tragedies. Remembering and forgetting, endless. Life, some call it. Endless loss. Not them. Not yet.
They have no idea what's ahead.*

I wrote that before. I got As in English, bitch.

See? I am literate.

It's not fair to show it now. So I'm told.

The lawyers call it proof of premeditation. Duh. You can't be best without planning first.

But it's good, huh? Literary. E V O C A T I V E. I should be the one writing the damn book. I should be the one getting rich. I was the one who knew those boys best. I could put words to their thoughts in ways they couldn't.

> *All that summer, hung over, gorged*
> *on the sun. Nights parked by the greasy lake.*
> *Nightswimming. Peeling, pulling*
> *leeches from my shin.*
> *Feeling alive. Alive.*
>
> *Plus I was a girl.*
> *Male. Male. Male.*
> *Student shooters.*
> *Boil, blackness. Holes.*
> *Female student shooter.*
> *Female shooter.*

Dash played the bass and Robbie was trying to learn guitar and then the drums. He kept switching back and forth. He said he couldn't decide, but I knew it was because he sucked at both. Not deciding, his way of deflecting. I was going to write the songs and sing. Right around then I started the notebook with the lines and lyrics and some of the shit I've remembered and copied down here. Even though there wasn't a thing those boys wouldn't do, sticking with something, seeing it through, well, except for the obvious, wasn't something they could do.

We would go to parties on Saturdays. The party masters had these made-up rules about the whole thing. You couldn't get in the door without a handful of pills to add to the bowl and you couldn't stay unless you took at least four at the door. They made up these fucked-up rules to get fucked up. We'd be up all night or fucked zombies trying to stay awake.

Rage, Rage
Bring on the dying of the light
Partying like it's 1999.
Most of us were born in 1999.

Dash had been in trouble at school. First for talking back to just about every teacher. Then chewing gum. Shooting rubber bands. Shooting wadded up paper from self-made rubber-band slingshots. Shooting hard chewed gum from a new slingshot because the other had been taken away. Trouble for drugs. And then fights. He'd knock the biggest guy into the lockers and play stupid, then do that every day to see how long it would take the idiot to take a swing.

Dash's dad was a doctor of some kind, not the medical kind. Ph doctor in physics or engineering or some other bright shit with equations. He's got this whiteboard in his office. Dash erased some symbols and drew penises in their place. Brainy asshole dude double bolted the door after that.

Dash's parents had him kidnapped and taken to a wilderness behavioral retreat. Dash called it Fix Me Camp, but said it didn't work. The camp couldn't work because he was perfect. Or so he said. He was always saying shit like that. At Fix Me Camp, Dash was made to hike out in the mountains and then set up camp around a lake. The boys were separated into different encampments far away from one another for three days of fasting and meditation.

If they left their site, it added time and chores to their stay at the Fix Me Lodge. If they didn't write in their journals, more time, more chores. Dash's journal looked something like this:

> *Loneliness, loneliness, boredom.*
> *Loneliness, loneliness, boredom.*
> *Loneliness, loneliness, boredom.*
> *Boredom. Boredom. Boredom.*
> *Pictures of boobs. Huge tits. Watermelons. Thighs.*
> *Food, food, food, food.*
> *I could eat the hell out of cheeseburger right now.*
> *Chocolate-ass milkshakes.*
> *I miss chocolate-ass milkshakes.*
> *More pictures—boobs, bombs, explosions.*
> *This shit is boring. B O R I N G.*
> *BORING into my brain.*
> *A hole in the head.*
> *Both heads. Pinprick my dick.*

Robbie's dad was a postal worker, but the kid did what his dad didn't / wouldn't / couldn't.

Another shrink visited today. Another one writing a book, as if that'll make a difference. Violence & The Teen Female Offender. Something like that. Guess you're on the hook, too. She said she'd be interviewing survivors. She's on leave from some place in Oregon called Harrington Gardens. Sounds nice, doesn't it? Prison in the garden. Flowers and ponds and toads. My secret garden. I never promised you roses or a garden. I'll never get there. My crime was too big. My age too old. I'll never get out.

The good People of Colorado have killed 101 people. All dudes. All for murder. But no one under 18. Banned for the kiddies by the court on high. So even though there is a death penalty it's de facto defunct. I'll be here for ages with some books and letters, Friday night TV, if I'm good. Popcorn in a plastic bowl if I'm better than good. What kind of life is that? What kind. The kind you never ever think will be yours.

The good People of Colorado, even after the last trailer park bust, wouldn't keep my mother with them, behind walls and bars. If they'd kept her, I'd have seen her. If they'd kept her, she would have had to stay clean. My mother and her needles and her fucking gross meth mouth. My mother buying and selling. Her body on the bathroom floor, whispering, 'I would rather shove this needle in my arm than be your mother.'

She was clean for ten months when I was nine. Bright and hopeful. We had Thursday visitations. And then we didn't. Those pock marks mocked me. They said, 'I chose this over you.' 17 when she had me. Look ma! Look what I've accomplished at the same age!

We make our beds, lie down with maggots.

I'm young, ahead of my time. 18 now. 17 when I did what I did. A junior. I had another year. Then what? College. No way. No money. No reason. No mother and a beat dead father. Why bother?

If you think I'm unique in my generation, think again.

Oh the binder! Oh the fun!

A therapist can spend hours on dreams, which can be

elaborate metaphors or emotional readouts of the day.
All the unresolved tensions of a life stacked up.
Whole sessions sinking into sleep-dreams or day-
dreams, but too much time spent with dreams means
the loss of immediacy of the connection in the room,
the hinge on which everything hangs.

There are no diseases only stories.
This is not true.

I used to want to think this, but the cases here
prove otherwise. People don't behave in the ways
I witnessed unless there's a root disease. A seventeen year-old male doesn't kill his parents and
then walk into his school, among his friends
and supportive teachers, and unload a semi-
automatic because he has a <u>story</u> that needs to be
reconsidered. Story is half-truth, fragmented truth.
The media bundle it into twenty-second sound
bites and four-word headlines. Particles that don't
cohere. There is no bundling, just fatigue.

*I'm at work, at the Taco Bell over on Dober Street, closing Friday
night. As I look around I realize I'm the only girl on shift. Four
dudes and me. If they wanted to, if they all agreed or if some of
them agreed and one left and the other stood off to the side unsure
but unwilling to intervene, they could do anything at all to me.
Anything they wanted. Rape me. Punch me. Burn me with plates
right out of the microwave. Whatever. Tie me up in the supply
closet. No one would know. Two in the morning on a Friday night.
The walls are concrete thick. Nobody would hear a thing.*

I shouldn't have to think about this shit.

Some kids have the kind of dads who take black-and-white photos of their own kids as babies, naked and getting washed in the tub or sink, then frame them and hang them in bathrooms or dens. Mine took the same pictures and posted them online for beer money. He drinks can after can in front of the TV. Works. Drinks. Works. Drinks. Lady Shrink calls this benign neglect. Lady Shrink calls this somewhat functional alcoholism. I call this bullshit. The dude has rolled over and given up. I call him Mr. Impotent.

Why are people the way they are?

> *A box of polaroids*
> *Limbs & light*
> *Light & limbs*

> *Parts which do not add up*
> *Do not make whole*

From today's binder fun:

> The universe of the teenager is a narcissistic one.
> It is shut-off, impregnable. The padlocked bedroom
> door as case in point. The NO ENTRY signs. Part choice.
> Part not. We reinforce the walls by supplying
> computers and phones, and soon all teens hear is one
> another's chatter with less and less input from adults,
> which primes them for psychosis, as every detail, every
> incident, gets blown into outrageous proportions.
> A strange look on a stranger's face.
> Being called Jim instead of James.
> A change in the weather.

All directed slights, all personal affronts. The universe of the teenager reflected in digital images and sound, both compressed to fit the format. Voices in the school hallway. Stories and elaborations. Bountiful imagination. Down to the very detail. And the details fading. The story thins as their worlds grow smaller.

Binder. Bind her.
De facto. Defunct.
No one will be taking me out.
Shrinky Dick's thinking—fragmented and fucked as mine.

I don't know when Rob and Dash started The Plan. Plan B. Abort them all, Dash said. I still don't know what made him so angry. He was a quick fuse. Sophomore year he started drinking more. Maybe that. He loved smashing glass against brick. Dash knew math and angles, like his dad, full of logic. He argued us into everything. People want an explanation. I can't give them one, at least not one they'll accept. Everything was going on at once. Testosterone. Testosterone. Goose. Emotional illogic. Mis-logic. Misfired moods. How do you explain?

It doesn't feel
Like I am living
My own life. It's
Someone else's entirely.

Random notes from the Binder of the Fucked Up Girl:

Heavy cell phone use in Sweden linked to brain tumors. Autism and ADHD rates increase with cell exposure.

Electromagnetic fields cause depression and suicide.
2000 nested case study of utility workers and suicide risk.
Cell towers on the tops of schools.
Cell towers on schools?
Low-level EMFs rupture cell membranes.
Constant electropollution stresses the nervous system.
The teenager is in endless fight or flight.
Chaotic cortisol disturbs sleep, thus mood, behavior.

The notes get messy from there, but there's something about the body and biophotons and radiation and frequencies that hurt and frequencies that heal.

Frequencies. Static on the line. My phone made me do it.

That Viktor Frankel book they make kids read in English or psychology class, the one that basically says no one can take you away from you. You decide your attitude and actions in any given moment. This thing happened and I lived. Awful things all the time and people go on. They go on or they don't.

Go on
Vaguely uneasy & empty

I'm not angry or despairing. I'm heavy. I feel heavy like a fat girl or something.

There wasn't a thing those boys wouldn't do. Including me. But that was never about me. Or pleasure. Or teen L O V E. Fucking was frank experimentation. Fucking was what we thought we should do before we die. Just in case. Just to know.

Rise up
Rise up Young
Lavinia
Sleep sleep sleep
My sister

Life is bizarre. Human consciousness. You ever look around just kind of frozen and stunned? All those middle class lawns and leafy smells. All those malls and stadiums. All those gadgets and widgets.

Lady Shrink talked about wifi waves and cellular signals. Same sort of bullshit Dash's dad was into. Something about the waves affecting our mitochondria. Our cells being hijacked and we can't see it, hear it, smell it, touch it, taste it, but the hijacking is happening. DNA. RNA. We are morphing into monsters. Electrical monsters.

I have been thinking of quitting. Thinking of these gray hallways versus the buoyancy of vacation voices and tanned, drunk faces careless and free. The mind has only so much capacity. The heart can only take so much. Compassion. Fatigue.

I am afraid of the sound of the words in my head.
I am afraid of the sound of the words of my voice.
I am afraid of the sound of the self who sounds within.
I am afraid of the self.
I am afraid.
I am.

What am I doing?
What are we doing?

Tell me
This

Why are things the way they are?
We are bio matter in an indifferent universe.

When I was seven or eight I used to lie in the bathtub with my legs
in the air so the water could pound down between my legs. I made
the water hot. I made it cold. Lady Shrink says the behavior is
natural, that it's normal for kids to explore their junk.

Ashamed of your beginnings
Grow recklessly ambitious to escape them
Latch to another's hatching plan

Forgiveness. No forgiving. No forgetting.
I live with this.
This. This. This. That. This. This.

I don't have an answer for anything.

Negligent discharge of a firearm.
Many arms.

This is what I read today:

The teenager lives in a superstitious world. The
teenager is hyperaware. Both conspicuous and
invisible. The teenager wants the world to be black
and white. Wants to be able to see that world as
black and white. But the world refuses to conform,

and comes at them and comes at them, and we step
out of the way.

Or in the way. Rob's way. Dash's.

*I know you want The Why. I know they give me these notebooks so
they can learn. A + B + C will make you feel better. As if anything
any of us does can be explained. As if we can be explained. A + B +
C will never equal anything.*

*I'm walking toward the inevitable, though uncertain and incurious
of what exactly that is, following it to the point where it disappears.
Ultimate mystery. Ultimately mysterious.*

> *Not tulips.*
> *The daffodils are too yellow.*
> *In the first place.*

> *You will have to live*
> *A life like any life*
> *There is no miraculous.*
> *There is the body's fast growth and decline.*

> *I want to be forgotten in the most*
> *unknown corner of the world.*

> *If they don't kill me I will kill myself now*
> *And then all of it will be behind us*

> *You see—*
> *It does finally*

ALL THAT IS BEHIND US NOW

All fall apart

All that is behind you now
Grows bright, a sunbaked memory
Of time without longing or loss
A time of the sun on the sand,
Your knees in the sand, sinking,
Your hands building,
Your body prostrate before
an impossible future.

Amanda Jane, fuck the last name.

MARRIAGE

During the first year of my parents' separation, my mother kept going off with strange men, sometimes for several hours, other times for several days, returning under-slept, clothes torn, missing an earring or bracelet. She'd drop into an hours-long stupor with her head tucked beneath the comforter and her body succumbing to the couch cushions. My dad, who solemnly and ineffectively drank through his grief, had moved into an apartment with a coworker. My dad was a mailman who lost his job after he ran his truck off a bridge and down the banks of the Little Miami. They say he hit his head, and that that was the reason for his odd behavior, but some part of me understood differently. After losing his job, he felt inept. He was home too much, and he shoved my mother once, who promptly told him to get out. She changed the locks that same night.

All of this happened after the wreck. I was eight when Gary and John didn't beat the train across the tracks. They were down in Florence for John's freshman football game. My parents had a work party that night. I was over at a friend's house. My parents didn't pick me up until way late the next day, and already they couldn't talk to each other. I hated Gary. He used to fold me in half, knees at my ears, pinning, compressing me until I couldn't breathe. Or he'd straddle me, his knees on my crucified arms, his face hovering over mine, a strand of saliva inching its way from his mouth toward my eye. John would tackle him and start a fight he couldn't win to get him to stop.

I understand all of the behavior better now—my mom's, my dad's, Gary's even, jealous of the attention the baby girl got, but I don't forgive it. I don't like most of the memories from my childhood. Sadness sweeps through me when I think of my lost eight-year-old little soul. I was an inquisitive, skipping kid, tormented by one brother and protected by the other, who grew into a confused and abandoned orphan. Sometimes I see my childhood as a form of preparation for these days with Liz.

After Gary and John's wreck and disappearance—the experience felt, at that age, as if they'd just vanished—after my father moved out, and just after I'd turned ten, my mother didn't earn enough as an aesthetician to make the house payment or to get an apartment for the two of us. Besotted with grief from the sudden loss of her first and second born, followed by the not-so-sudden demise of her marriage, she became an unfit mother. She relinquished me to foster care for a year, or so she promised. "It's just for a little while, Abigail."

That was the last time I saw her.

Dale, Diane, and David Fredrickson lived in a small, weathered house in the lower-income area of Hyde Park. Diane, who chain-smoked Marlboro Lights and wore stonewashed jeans and tight sweaters, had married young to Dale, a car mechanic and amateur mixed-martial-arts fighter. They had a son, David, twelve, who was nothing like either of them. He was sensitive and artsy. He liked to draw cartoons and listen to jazz. Dale gave David boxing lessons, using gloves when he'd been drinking beer and bare fists when he'd been drinking whiskey. I used to clean David's broken skin with peroxide if it was available or vodka if his mother had passed out before the bottle's end.

David and I didn't talk to each other at first. Sliding into his skateboard phase, he busied himself mowing lawns to save eighty dollars for a deck, trucks, and wheels, then another eighty for shoes and black shirts. He spent hours in the driveway, practicing ollies and kick-flips, spinning one-eighties. The sound of board against concrete mesmerized me. My brothers were all balls and rough play. Skating was street ballet. I sat on the back steps, watching David kick down, rise, land. Kick down, rise and flip, land. Kick down, catch the toe wrong, stumble, fall. Curse, repeat. Exhausted or frustrated by his lack of skill with the board, he'd go inside and lie on the floor in his room and draw cartoons on the backs of used envelopes because his parents wouldn't buy him a sketch-pad. He'd toss his mistakes and file away sketches he liked in a shoe box. Then, growing restless again, his young body unable to tolerate long bouts of stillness, he'd go back outside.

At my first house, life revolved around the boys and football, football, football. Baseball kept them moving in the springtime. John secretly told me he preferred baseball because of the sun on the field and the smell of cut grass. That, and he didn't have to hit or tackle or be hit and be tackled. Short and brutish, Gary thrilled to anything football. He was a bull. My dad loved his energy and showed his pride with annoying, embarrassing, and regular chest bumps. I was not a boy, and I was not football, and therefore my father had no idea what to do with me. My mother kept to the salon. Her best clients showed up between three and eight. And so, even before the wreck, I felt unplaced, unmoored in my own family.

I watched David, as I'd watched my brothers, and tried to figure him out. He was nothing like Gary. He was a little like John. Both had a kindness to them at that age. David was closer to my age than either of my brothers had been, so maybe we had more in common. Or maybe we grew to rely on each other out of necessity. We were all the other had. Because he didn't have to compete with a sibling, David developed his own interests free of familial influence. His parents' benign and aggressive neglect forced him to entertain and soothe himself. "Ferberized until 15," he would later say.

In the Fredrickson house, I battened my lips and made myself small, a difficult feat because I'd had a growth spurt. New height, new hips, new breasts. David's dad wanted me to play basketball, and I suppose I would have, had he or Rita paid the team fees. They forgot a lot, drank a lot, fought a lot. Dale never hit his wife and only knocked me aside a couple of times. He was mostly an emotional, psychological abuser. David took the worst of Dale's moods and unhappiness, an open hand to the head, swung from a drunken arm.

David, my keeper of secrets and infinite sadness.

I had a slippery hold on the "little while" I was supposed to spend in foster care. A little while with no end. Just until mom gets herself together. In the meantime, in the meanwhile, keep waiting, stay quiet and out of the way. Be helpful when present. In high school a few years later, I read Beckett in an English class. During my three interminable years in the Fredrickson house, I'd learned how to wait, except I wasn't waiting for Godot, just for my mother who never came. Instead, my father collected me, shaking Dale's hand firmly, as if they'd closed on the sale of a used car. Dad took me to his sister, Maureen, explaining that my mom had allowed herself some fun with needles and was in a court-appointed rehab center. He had found work as a distance trucker. He'd send money and see me when he could. I'd be staying with Maureen. He barely hugged me when he left.

Maureen, whom I called Ree when I first learned to talk, had an apartment in Clifton, not too far from the university. She bedecked her four hundred square feet with weird posters, incense, and layers of rugs. She owned volumes of books and art-house movies. She let me watch or read whatever I wanted, regardless of the content, claiming I'd discover smut and beauty and violence someday one way or another. To live with her, I had to change schools again to somewhere too far away to spend regular time with David. I befriended books and music. With so much change and turmoil, you accustom yourself to solitude. You stop expecting things, or you slit your wrists a thousand different ways.

My father acutally had two siblings, but the brother, two years his junior died of leukemia at twelve. Ree arrived unexpectedly nine years later. "It was like my parents had two families, Ted and Keith, then me and the yapping dog. Ted was more like a distant uncle or an estranged family friend." But they kept in touch and Ree always liked my mom. If my dad was football, then Ree was dance. She trained from a young age and could have made a career in modern ballet. She toured seasonally with a company, and had spent time in Chicago and Los Angeles, where she was offered a permanent position. But she declined and returned to Cincinnati after the car wreck. She blew her twenties on me. She worked at her former studio and drove me around to school, the orthodontist, counseling appointments. For years I felt that I had held her back. Then David pointed out, "If she was supposed to go, she would have found other arrangements for you. She was twenty-four and worldly. She was capable of making moves if she wanted to make them and if they were there to make. She wasn't the first one asked." My guilt was *my* guilt. Ree didn't seem disconsolate about missing the limelight, nor did she seem unhappy as my guardian. David again, "You gave purpose to a decade that's otherwise hazy memories of bars and regrettable hookups."

"*Your* twenties maybe."

"Yours, too!"

David's memory falsely included me in his three a.m. theft of a kid's sled from his yard—"His fault for not stowing it away!"—and his memory of wandering through the Queen of Hearts, a sex club in Kentucky. So selective, David's recall. He liked to blank out my three years with Alexandra, obliterating her existence, let alone her importance to me. In college, misfit for the sporty dykes, the theatre screwballs, the spoken-word coffeehouse dwellers, I stayed late at the library or conferred with professors after class. Shims of light slipped in. Conversations led me to Diane Arbus, Richard Sandler, Robert Mapplethorpe. You can't live in Cincinnati and not confront Mapplethorpe. A wallflower, I opened more under Alexandra's attention. Five years older and a teaching assistant in my women's literature class, Alexandra was working on an MFA. A little moody, she'd shut herself up in her apartment for three days, unplug her phone, and blacken the windows to labor on her thesis. She emerged grungy and shy, blinking at the light, wanting to go hiking in Hocking Hills or spelunking in Mammoth Caves. She was of a generation that took art seriously, or at least took herself seriously enough to pursue an art-centered life. Art held power for her, as did words. She wanted to change the face of American poetry. I thought she just might. I know better now, about the difference between desire and achievement. I understand there's nothing new to find on the backside of the sun, just more sun.

I learned from Alexandra that distance doesn't necessarily mean dislike or disdain, nor even avoidance. Distance does not mean you are worthless or fundamentally flawed and that the relationship is over. It could indicate simply a need to study, to do work, to partake of solitude for renewal or insight. No agendas. No judgment. No secrecy. No betrayal.

Prior to Alexandra, my adventures included a few under-the-clothes fumblings with David, a make-out session with a boy in a car in high school, and a night of spin-the-bottle that had me kissing the school prom queen several times. Rendered relationship-phobic by my parents' split and the Frederickson's dysfunction, I'd never been boy-crazy, nor imagined a wedding day or future husband. What brought people together and made them nuts mystified me on a fundamental level.

Alexandra's love of language, her need to tell a story well or capture an emotion in an image, made me think I might like to write or do the same through photographs. I leeched her energy for several weeks, even going so far as buying a camera. An hour's drive from campus, was an old, huge, abandoned Victorian house, four floors, shelving everywhere foot to ceiling, crammed with books upon books, spines out. A labyrinth of ideas on every subject imaginable. Literature rolled into art and huge coffee table books and zigzagged from the second to the third floor. The futility of ambition swept through me as I walked the haphazard stacks. I stopped. Breathless. Trapped.

I didn't want to compete and I knew that I couldn't. I didn't want to drive myself mad, hiding away for days, pretending to create something defensible. I didn't need to be anybody or prove anything. I didn't write. I didn't take more pictures. I learned to be content, even moved, by other peoples' efforts. The world contained enough words, pictures, paintings, poems, videos without mine added to the scree.

And according to David, the world didn't need Alexandra's output either. Six years after our faux family togetherness, David and I reconnected in college, running into each other after a philosophy seminar. Attempting to get out of the city of his childhood, away from his parents, he'd spent an unhappy year at Bowling Green where he'd followed a girl, ended up having sex with a boy, then returned to Cincinnati distraught and as confused as ever. His confusion abated when he learned I was living part-time with a girl, at which point he, without anguish, teeter-tottered between sexes. Four months with a man, six with a woman. Nine months, seven. Eighteen, two. Charles lasted longest, but I wasn't sure he counted since David, for Charles, was a satellite relationship.

Initially, Alexandra tried to be friendly with David. He threw nothing but hostility at her. "You're wearing that?" "You only have tea in this house? Tea is for cat-ladies and band singers." Alexandra was a quick study. She stopped responding to his insults, stopped offering herself as a target. He'd taunt her, at any hour, drumming on the door, yelling, quoting, "C'mon Alex, 'There will be time and motive enough to prose on about your life when you have generated, as it were, a sufficient cloud of reflection,' but for now, let's go find us some trouble, let's go dancing." At that time in my life, just

as I'd tried to write and tried some photography, I tried dancing and staying out late. I tried smoking pot and protesting
wars. Tried to be a participant. I went looking for my true self
wherever I could find her.

A year later, Alexandra finished her degree, and, fancying
herself an Anne Carson, she left me for a PhD in Classics in
Boulder. I could never tell if her writing was good. Mostly I
didn't understand it. That she had moved to Cincinnati and
then again three years later to a farther, colder city astonished
me. Boulder seemed far away and exotic to a girl who'd never
traveled west of Bloomington, south of Lexington, or north of
Dayton. Overjoyed to see her go, David said, "I don't know
what you ever saw in her. She's a pouty, privileged, know-it-
all. And her poetry sucks hairy balls."

During our mid-twenties, David worked summer construction until he drove a nail through his left foot, joining a small
part of himself to a suburban deck. "Thanks sub-sis," he said,
as I drove him home from the emergency room. He was high
on pain meds. "Sub-sis. You help me subsist. Sub cysts."

"You're not a substitute, David. You're my brother. My only
brother."

David's foot healed and he disappeared. Except for the occasional postcard, I didn't hear from him for three years. He
went back to Bowling Green, studied psychology and literature, before debarking for nursing school in Chicago—not an
easy gig, being a male nursing student in the Midwest. People
wondered what his story was, an uncertainty that prevented
him from getting a local job. He signed on as a contract nurse
and traveled wherever they sent him. Wisconsin, Texas, Al-
abama, Hawaii, Alaska. He'd swing back through Cincinnati

between jobs and stay with Ree and me or just with me after I rented a place of my own. David liked Honolulu, the lush landscape, the sun. I liked getting his postcards, but not the visit from the FBI one of them occasioned. As a traveler and outsider, David didn't have routines, places to go, people to meet, so he started reading and writing in earnest. He'd found Kathy Acker and Dennis Cooper. He'd copy out passages and send them to me. The Cooper postcard had lines from *Wrong*, involving what seemed to be blatant child molestation. A postal worker had alerted the FBI.

After he became a nurse, David began to care for himself a little better. He stopped eating fast food and drinking soda. He rarely stayed out past one and frequented community center yoga and tai chi classes. And, as he calls it, he entertained some semi-serious talk therapy.

"Here's the test. When you are miserable, what is your impulse? Do you call someone immediately or do you sit on the couch and gaze out at nothing? You, you're the gazer. I'm the connector."

"Basic difference between introvert and extrovert," I said. "Or worldviews. One fundamentally believes there will always be someone around. The other believes we are ultimately all alone."

"Optimist versus pessimist. The realist splits the difference."

David was sad that night, and sadness in him translated to drinking or some other madness that lasted all night. I, too, was sad at that time, having recently watched another girlfriend move away, so I played along with David's psychosis.

"It's all flash without the jazz. Did you know 'jazz' derives from jism or dinza and really means to ejaculate?" He'd been dating a linguistics major. "Why do you live here? This town is like an Alice Munro story. Nothing happens."

"This again? You want to fake-argue about Munro of all things?"

Getting to what's troubling David takes time and patience, elliptical conversation, and not an insignificant amount of whiskey.

"Let's get funky. Where can we go? Did you know 'funky' originally meant positive sweat? Like from dancing or the sheen of sweat when fucking? I tell you, language is ruined by people, completely corrupted. And boogie meant devilishly good." After being dumped, David had stolen the linguistic major's Adderall and swallowed three of them before coming to see me.

"What's really bothering you?"

"It doesn't matter. They're all temporary."

"That's never bothered you before."

He waved me off and we sat in rare silence. Mr. Linguistics held something special to which David no longer had access.

"James Robert Baker," David said, and I tried to ignore him, but he was like a jumpy, irritated three-year-old if he didn't get his way. "C'mon. James Robert B."

"Okay. R. Rothko up the forearm."

"Oll out the window."

"Who the hell is that?"

"Chess grandmaster."

"Laake. Pills."

"Enke. Train."

"Sports? Really?"

"Recent. The boys tell me these things. What's your excuse?"

"Soccer's the rage in the Midwest. Ernest."

"Boring."

"Shotgun. Still counts."

"Tilson comma Henry. Shot to the heart."

"Nearing. The rarest of the rare, starvation."

"Brutal. Spalding Gray."

"That one still hurts my heart."

David and I had pilgrimaged to the Beaumont in 1994 for *Gray's Anatomy* and again two years later for *It's a Slippery Slope*. We sat attuned to NPR for updates when Gray went missing, and we ran around buying his books after his body surfaced in the East River.

"Mine, too."

Empedocles dove into Etna, Plath into her oven. Woolf filled her pockets with rocks and walked into a river. Celan? A different river. Nerval hung himself with apron strings. David Wallace with a sturdy rope in the… I don't know which room. Garage? Jack London, morphine. In this game, sometimes we go chronological. Sometimes we make a name-game of it, the next name using the last letters of the first or last name. Sometimes we shift, and for every real suicide David matches it to a fictional one.

Ophelia, Goneril, Cleopatra.

He loves Shakespeare.

"Chatterton with arsenic," I said.

"You always try Chatterton, but he doesn't count since it's unclear if his death was an accident. He had syphilis and could have been trying to cure it."

"Unlikely."

"Even so. Next!"

"Chesnutt."

"Now you're being mean and trying to make me sad," David said.

We could play the game for hours, making tragedy and suffering our chew toys.

"Cobain, then, gun. Or drugs. I can't remember."

"He doesn't count," David said. "He wasn't a poet. He was a junky rock star."

This was how the game went. I never won because David was the master of the rules, and the rules constantly changed.

"You let sports in. We aren't talking just poets and writers."

I used to think more about suicide, both as a means and an end. As something I could do if need be, if I got desperate or didn't care or just didn't want to participate any longer. Escapist thinking, yes, but also seriousness wrapped in curiosity and philosophy. Suicide as a final act of freedom and self-agency. Don't misinterpret me. I'm not exiting. A palm-reader once told me I'll live to ninety-three, an active ninety-three. I'm curious to see if he was correct.

"Should I worry?" I asked David.

He pulled my head to his and kissed me on the cheek. "Never."

Gary, John, my parents, those women, all in the past, many miles ago. Things matter only if you let them. Leave them behind. That was my bumper-sticker philosophy. I read for two decades straight, not wanting to proceed bewildered and afraid through my twenties and thirties. I preferred to be seen as steady, dull, maybe a little aloof. Even uptight would do. I followed through on commitments. I showed up when I said I would. I avoided attention and contented myself with routines and rules—up at seven, coffee and the paper, a light breakfast.

Wash the dishes immediately. Walk to a gallery or museum, read. Work at two. Containment was key. Not many do well with true freedom. I accorded myself with rhythm and simplicity, with serial, albeit short, relationships, and visits or holidays with Ree and David. My family was small and my life fit neatly into a five-mile radius.

David, who was friends with the youngest Gimo son and washed dishes at the restaurant, introduced me to Akhiro, the patriarch and owner, who gave me a job as a hostess and then let me manage the place eighteen months later when his wife died and he took her body back to Japan for burial. In addition to the restaurant, I also managed Akhiro's three sons. After two years I earned their respect and we steadied our paces. And that was my life. Read, work, walk, look at art, read, work, visit with David, visit with Ree.

And then my routines and contentment and ideas about a quiet life got torn down.

And then all I thought about love and romance and sex and intimacy and what went into a good life was bankrupted.

And then my walking and reading and looking and working felt like extinction.

Because there was Liz.

When we are at our zenith, we exude confidence, feel a secure hold on the world, our own small world. We feel so large, so right, that we become attractive to others and attract good toward us. That's why employment counselors suggest not leaving a job when you're feeling lousy about the work, irritated by the people, and disgruntled about your status. Better to interview when you're thriving, selling, balancing, when everyone looks toward you with envy and admiration. Liz was operating on just such an apex when I met her. She had finished her post-graduate internship at the university medical center and had hired into a staff position. With a wage she could actually live on, she was searching for an apartment of her own. She had purchased a car. All she needed was The Girl.

Enter Abigail Connelly. Calm, quiet, older, possessed of none of Elizabeth Daubman's youthful ambition. I was stunned when Liz came back to the restaurant after I had thrown her out. Stunned, but also amused. Fresh, thirty, bold, she exuded a college air—grad school, but dignified on the cheap and earnest. She hadn't yet surrendered her youth. She wasn't beaten down or resigned like some of the women I'd dated. Sad internet interludes, those. Liz wore skinny black jeans and a tight white V-neck from which her cleavage winked. A few bracelets jangled on her wrist. She had Patti-Smith hair that she swept from her eyes throughout the night. We sat on barstools facing each other, and I struggled to keep my hand off her thigh.

For a long time, I hid that I was smitten. Liz would tell you otherwise. I clung to my routines, despite my longing to disrupt them with her. I enforced separate time. I never called in sick for a day in bed with her, nor bailed on an exercise class. Liz was young after all, and I was sure, despite all her contraindications that she'd grow bored and move along to someone younger. At no point did she squirrel away feelings she had for me. I suppose my face betrayed me. She looked as stunning in skinny jeans and tight shirts as she did in a skirt or naked. She felt as good strapped in on top of me as she did on her hands and knees in front of me. She smelled enticing. She tasted delicious. I had never entertained the idea of such idiot joy. I had planned to be content. I'd weathered enough emotional extremes for a lifetime—enough loss, enough confusion. So I trundled off to Pilates and to work, yet still she persisted, showing up for dates she'd planned, sending flowers to the restaurant, leaving me coy notes in current books. I'd never been pursued so forthrightly. Nor had I dated anyone younger. Youth meant bars and beers and petty hook-ups. Youth meant late nights, early mornings, too much TV and texting, concerts and Ikea furniture, dirty neck tattoos, uncontained emotions, and entitled digital wizards who thought moneymoneymoney and remained naively upbeat despite high unemployment and massive student loan debt. But Liz honored her commitments and left her phone at home. Her skin was free of ink. She only had two piercings, one in each ear. Dear Liz, young and fresh and unrestrained.

I have never been the type of person to make quick friends in bars or skin the ears of acquaintances. Nor have I ever sat on a stool, nodding along, a docile and captivated audience. I am the type who pays attention for eight full minutes and half a drink, then excuses herself at the first opportunity. Any longer and my torso swells with an emptiness that can't be rocked away, expanding with each minute passing. Liz, on the other hand, starts conversations with strangers. "Spring break for you? I've been wondering why there are so many little people on the flight." "Have a good trip?" "What do you do for work?" "Oh, I'm not much into sports, but Seattle folks do love their Seahawks. Those guys, football players, are in good shape. Too bad about all the head injuries."

Liz had lived a charmed life. The middle child of three, each two years apart. Catholic school and Sunday dresses. Vacations to Disney World, Myrtle Beach, Niagara Falls. An affluent home. Summer camps and cello lessons. Her sisters graduated from medical school. "Book-ended by doctors," she sighed. Her mother, a lawyer who practices family law, tends to divorces and property disputes, custody and child support. Alimony. Pre-nups. Post-nups. Ugly business, but she tried as best she could to make a positive difference in the lives of crumbling families. Liz's father had been a math teacher, then a principal, then a district administrator. Education suffused the household, and not as a privilege, nor a means of escape. Despite all this rectitude, Liz turned out all right. She could just as easily talk about Barnett Newman as computer code as Marilyn Hacker. She talked a lot, but she didn't have much to say about her youth.

"I didn't do anything worth mentioning until I got to college. 4.2 GPA, a small scholarship. Away from home for the first time, forging my own identity. I wrote what I thought were risqué essays. 'Lesbian Signification in *My Antonia* and Alice Austen's Photographs.' 'Bondage Imagery in Dickinson's Poems.' One semester I shaved my head and wore black bras and white T-shirts everywhere."

"Scandalous."

"Totally. A true rebel." She laughed at herself. "That's what college is for, right? Exploration and change. Thinking. Trying out different personas. My older sister wasn't like me. She steered right toward a career track. She spent four years in labs and lecture halls. She had no idea who she was nor how to relate to people when the four years were done. Mark my words, midlife crisis coming for that girl, and not a small one either. Met her husband while doing experiments on mice. Sexy, huh? Married a month after graduation." She paused and considered me. "I do want marriage. I want to commit to one person and experience dailyness. I'm done experimenting and having flings. I know what that life is. Adrenaline rush after adrenaline rush. Living an addiction. It lacks depth and longevity. You're eerily quiet, Abby."

"Just listening."

"And you?"

"I've never wanted to marry."

"I figured as much."

"Do you still play the cello?" I asked.

"Occasionally."

"Play it for me."

"Only if I'm naked."

David didn't favor Liz, but he always dumped on anyone I dated, even if he hadn't yet met the person. But as much as David disliked Liz, Ree liked her ten times more.

"You should marry that girl."

"We're different."

"What two people aren't? Do you have key values in common?"

"Yes."

"Does she listen when you talk?"

"Yes."

"Do you listen when she talks?"

"Yes."

"Do you laugh? Is the sex decent?"

"Yes, yes, but there are thirteen years between us."

"Do you hear yourself?"

"All right, already."

After I'd moved out of her apartment, Ree bought a small one-bedroom house in Mariemont. She liked the English architecture of the neighborhood and said the area was the closest thing to living abroad that she could afford. She continued to teach dance and had even choreographed a small show with a performer named Jersey whom she'd dated for almost a decade. The show played in a drafty, renovated warehouse that could assemble forty people in an oval around the stage, which was level with the seating. Ree called the show *Strand*. The dancers wore pastel leotards with tails and streamers of cloth. Nine of them toed circles, spirals, squares, pearls of string. The shapes formed and dissolved in a nuanced blend, patterning with string music. Just as a dancer seemed to come together with another in a duet, a darting off would erupt, a charging into the air. Dancers launched into impossible splits, then landed dissonantly far from the audience. The light meanwhile slapped about, thick and inky, in sudden slices. *Strand* ended as if incomplete. Some dancers simply stopped in place, some walked away, some dropped to the floor. They held position until the audience, confounded, uncertain, dispersed.

In addition to dance, Jersey had studied physics . He'd read to Ree from Feyman, Hawking, and Gribbin. Jersey liked to say that we're all bags of photons and the best dance reveals the hidden structure of cell signaling. "Read Becker. We're hot wires. We're electrical." Jersey crackled with theories and made connections across the sciences and the arts. He was often hard to follow.

Companionable, always teasing and touching each other with their lithe dancers bodies, Ree and Jersey were well-paired. I thought they would die together after decades in a condo in Ft. Lauderdale, but they broke up during the final week of the show. Jersey, nearing sixty, had had sex with the seventeen-year-old lead female dancer. Ree said she could have overlooked what he'd done. She had before. "All my relationships are open. It's fallacy to think we can be contented with one person for forever." She had on occasion wandered herself. "It's messy and incestuous with other dancers, certainly, but you high half-toe through that minefield. What I cannot abide is that she's a child. A tight hole and smooth skin, all right, I can understand the attraction. But a child? No. Wait for twenty-five or choose someone else." Ree, self-professed serial monogamist, had never married, but always wanted me to. "Make some vows. Commit to a way of life."

Marriage. I didn't care at all about it. "I *am* committed to a way of life, probably much more than other people."

"Marriage signifies stability and maturity."

"Nonsense. Billions of unstable, immature people get married. Marriage is limitation and restraint. It's a fence for fear. You realize your argument holds no water?"

"Marriage has nothing to do with true love and everything to do with choice. Besides, we are not talking about what's right for me. Most people expect too much from marriage. It used to be a power arrangement in the upper classes and people's needs were met by a whole community, but it's not like that anymore. You'll like it. You're a realist. You'll feel differently once you've tied the knot. Marriage will suit you."

"*Tie the knot?* Just like a noose. Look, I've had women come in and out of my life. I've had experiences. They run their course. You collide with someone for whatever reason, hover, then drift. I'm content with that. You understand."

"Abby, you and Liz have been together for four years."

I couldn't argue anymore. I had nothing left with which to counter. Liz worked and played, and I read and worked. We traveled around America to National Parks and museums. We ventured to Ireland and France and sunbaked Greece. We made plans for the Great Wall. We traveled easily together and didn't mind afternoons apart. Hours could swim by with the two of us reading on opposite ends of the couch. We slept well side by side. I didn't mind being dragged to jazz nights or lame one-woman shows. I survived the yearly office party and claustrophobic Thanksgivings with her family. Liz rode a strong energy, enough for the two of us, which swelled beneath and around us, filled the space with dazzling happiness. At year six, I'd decided I didn't want anyone else. And in year eight, luckily, we married. We married after all. We married right in time.

LONG PATIENCE

We had married in time. I was notified when Liz was on the helicopter headed to Bayview General. I was taken to the ICU without questions or second looks. I was deferred to as next-of-kin and wielded medical power-of-attorney. I would say when treatment would cease and I would sign off on the donation of her organs if it came to that. I would be in charge of decisions and arrangements. The doctors didn't think her situation so dire, but they had to allow for all possibilities. They had to prepare. So did I.

"There's been an incident," they'd said on the phone. "We'll explain when you get here. Take your time. Drive slowly or get a cab. She's not here yet and will be in surgery shortly after she arrives."

"Surgery?"

"We'll explain when you arrive. Go to the ICU."

Liz's cell clicked to voicemail when I called, eight times in my disbelief and confusion.

Of course I rushed, exceeded all speed limits, cut people off, tried unsuccessfully to thwart panic: my wife is dying, my wife is dead, something's happened to my wife.

"She was stabilized on-scene by medics and taken to the closest hospital, where they removed the bullets. As you can guess, first-responders were overwhelmed by the number of cases pouring in. Given her perforated bowel and the state of her pelvis, they opted to fly her here. We had no idea she was local until I called your number. Lucky for you, you didn't have to travel far."

Lucky me.

"She'll be in 902 after surgery. You can wait in the room or take a walk, get some coffee. I'll call you when she's out. It may be awhile. Perforations can take time."

Not the worst outcome. She's alive after a terrible, unreal day. Her brain continues to function on its own as does her heart. Her reflexes are intact. I had imagined darker scenarios: death, maiming, disability. Imagining is a form of preparation. Catastrophizers make better copers because their minds have pre-survived the minefields. I'd envisioned Liz crushed within a car, lost from contact on a backcountry ski trip, aloft in a plane that bursts an engine, plunging off narrow hiking trails, not to mention bike wrecks, broken arms, crushed feet. What I did not imagine were the tubes, the cords, the technology tied to the body, nor the bandages and portals and drainage. I had not imagined the serious lights and the influx of strangers coming for their intimate tasks. Not the sense of helplessness. Not the survival and the what-now. The films and labs. The waiting. The words. Bowel, bullets, pelvic fixation.

We had married in time. I was at her side day and night. The staff didn't request that I step out when they cleaned her wounds or checked her reflexes or emptied her bags. They kept me informed. They asked if I was okay. They brought me water and a blanket. They explained the procedures and tubes and machines. They tried to tell jokes. *What does Tickle Me Elmo get before leaving the factory? Two test tickles.* They patted my arm. They left me alone with the female chaplain in polyester pants that didn't hide her thigh-chub, which I fixated on as mottled clay, long misshapen lumps.

"It will be okay, and you will both get through this," she said.

"God has a plan even if we can't see it," she said.

"We could read from the scriptures, if you like," she said.

"It's a terrible tragedy," she said. "That school, those poor families."

"Take solace. She's in God's good hands," she said.

"If there's anything I can do, please let me know," she said.

"You're strong. The doctors here are so good."

"Have patience," she said. "God will reveal all in due time."

"Stop talking," I said.

"Are you from a different denomination? Because if so, that's okay. God hears us all," she said.

"Just stop talking."

I was not from a different denomination. I had no denomination. I had on occasion allowed myself verbal playtime with believers. After all and obviously, scripture was a text fallibly written by humans decades after the deaths of alleged prophets. Why would an omnipotent deity ply us with falsity? How can benevolence accommodate progeria or childhood leukemia? Alzheimer's? Or Huntington's? Bad things happened to people, good and not-so-good, all the time without pattern, without reason, or wisdom. To those who recommended faith, I gave a stare or a laugh.

Within the hospital's cream-white and thickened walls, adorned with innocuous art, I sat in a floral cushioned chair and felt the loss of a mother. I wanted desperately to call one, ostensibly mine, but not because mothers always say the right thing or know exactly what to do. The mother I envisioned knew how to share sorrow. She would sit on the other end of the line in quiet knowing. That in itself would be more than enough. I had called Ree, my guardian, my protector, but she wasn't a mother. She hadn't given birth to me or anyone, and she didn't have the internal longing for children that other women profess. She couldn't share my sorrow, not how I wanted her to or thought I needed and missed. I had also called Liz's mom, but *her* daughter was on the gurney, and so she couldn't be for me what I needed. I sat alone in my longing those first hours.

Utilitarian architecturally and psychologically, the waiting rooms, while small, were not private. No one could be left alone for long. Strangers in grief stepped in and sat for some minutes and left again to pace or find answers or to rescue themselves from situations in which they were drowning. The longest to stay in the room was a young mother. Her son, who had been riding a mountain bike, collided with an ATV on a trail an hour outside of Seattle. The ATV rider broke an arm but was otherwise okay. The son sustained massive head trauma.

"Brain-dead," the woman said. "He was wearing a helmet. I made sure of that. That was supposed to be enough, right? Seventeen. I have to make the decision to shut down the venti-lator. You never think about these things when you have a kid, or maybe you do, but you never think they'll happen to you. Not really. I'm sorry to go on and on." She looked toward me. "Who are you here for?"

"My wife."

"She alive? She gonna make it?"

"Last I heard."

"Good, good for you. Where's your family? My family's all out there. I don't want to see them. Their grief. Their pity faces. The cards and flowers and all the fucking food that's gonna follow. People mean well, I know, but still. I hate lasagna. Cheese does a number on my gut."

She had skipped a stage of the Kubler-Ross quintet and had gone straight to anger. Rightly so. The natural order had been reversed. She was supposed to die before her son, and not for another forty years. As I listened to her, I thought of my parents in the hospital, facing down the simultaneous loss of two sons. I imagined the shock and tears and despair. At eight years old, I was spared an unfamiliar and harrowing hospital visit. I'd known nothing of sterile rooms and labyrinthine halls, the helpless faces and professional condolences. I'd never been in a hospital, not in fifty-plus years. That's some luck.

What I remember now from the hospital is a bright blur of beeps and needles and drainage. Nurses in colorful scrubs. Hurried doctors and their trailing interns. A machine breathing for Liz, inflating her lungs, the chest expanding, widening, followed by a slow collapse, a sinking. Rising, sinking. A perfect rhythm while she hibernated in a weighty drug-induced slumber, while her mind danced lightly in yellow fields of memory or not at all. Researchers say the normally lit areas in the brain are dark during coma while the dark regions are lit. Networks of neural pathways reorganize and Liz's hidden self would be mapped, connected, absolved at last. I reminded myself that Liz had not hit her head. Her face, yes, the cheekbone near the eye socket, but while her face looked like an oversized, discolored marshmallow, her brain had not swelled. She had all the oxygen she needed anywhere she needed it. She could be pulled out of her coma at any point. The benevolent anesthesiologist held the key.

What does Elmo get? Two testicles. Test tickles. Pain and tickle travel the same nerve pathway. You laugh at a tickle because your brain is trying to make sense of the sensation of pain coming from the touch of someone you otherwise trust.

Beyond the random facts and attempts to distract, what I remember from the hospital is an awful gurgling when a nurse cleaned Liz's breathing tube. The efficient nurse sent water into the tube that was bringing Liz air. Water. My wife—waterboarded. I held my breath as Liz, gurgling, choking, drowning, coughed and sputtered yet slept and dreamed of typhoons and tsunamis. I remember strangers propping her on her right side for an hour. Propping her toward the left. Raising the bed to seventy degrees. Laying it flat. Stuffing pillows all around her, bolstering her with cotton covered in washable plastic. Beeps and needles and drainage. Me, standing by, sitting at her side, talking to her, touching her, goading her away from golden light, coercing her not to give in to the false neuronal firing that suggested tunnels and pathways to the warm energy of dead loved ones. Me, waiting, Liz, lying there, where time had stopped.

After the sepsis in her gut was contained, after her pelvis was stabilized and no more surgeries were required, they brought Liz, my Lizarus, back to us. Her eyes, growing larger with panic, darted around the room. Her heart rate shot up in a succession of fast beeps until her eyes found mine and her whole body relaxed on the bed. The waiting was not over then. We could not simply go home and resume our lives. We spent a few more days on that floor before she was clear of infection

and clots. Liz had to be able to get herself into a sitting position before she could move on to rehab for more shifting and
sitting, self-care, building endurance and the strength required
to move without standing from bed to chair. Liz wasn't to support herself on her right leg for twelve weeks. Twelve weeks
of stuttered movements and shots of pain.

When we came home, she kept silent, as if she'd sworn a
vow. Not completely silent. She cried a lot the first several
days. She gasped and moaned when changing positions and
then later when starting to walk again, her right leg halting,
shuffling. She slept a lot. She used to be a four-to five-hour-
per-night sleeper. Up late, up early. Inexhaustible, strong energy propelled her. She enjoyed her work and was pleased with
herself and her career. She dressed in fresh, sharp lines, favor-
ing skirt-suits despite Seattle's bent toward the casual. Home
from work, she flitted about from computer to phone to me
to computer, chatting about projects, coworkers, inept bosses,
about powerless Seattle voters. "Want light rail connecting
West Seattle and downtown? Yes, yes, yes. No light rail.
Want a new stadium? No, no, thank you. Here you go: giant
stadium. Want a tunnel built within soggy tide flats and the
wooden rubble of old Seattle? No. Great! Here's your tunnel! Never mind the cost. We've already started digging! This
country isn't a democracy. Why did we ever think it was?" In
earnest, she could discuss Diane Arbus, her possible contem-
porary subjects. Liz knew the way to my heart, the way to keep
me. I had stopped voting at thirty-seven during the second
Bush administration. America was on a steep decline then.
The 2016 election, joke that it was, only greased the asphalt.
As private-minded as it was, I preferred to contemplate Edward Weston's *Pepper* side-by-side with Mapplethorpe's Ajitto
photographs, and thereby be comforted with quiet stillness.

Liz's newfound stillness, however, frightened me. She spent hours silent on the deck. Then she'd roll through the day: bedroom, hallway, bathroom, hallway, kitchen, hallway, office. Her world contained in twelve hundred square feet of hardwood and an ocean view. Watching Liz's slow progress, seeing her catch a wheel on flooring transitions and not be able to budge forward, watching and not assisting, was for me a brutal exercise in patience and restraint.

She kept the shades drawn, the TV off, the radio, her computer, prior lifeline, off. Her phone, too. She made small laps around the inside of the house. She sat on the deck. I worried. I waited for her words to pour forth. I waited for my brazen Liz to re-emerge. I paced the floors, as if doing so would reveal what should be done. We were both shocked and numb, though gratitude overlay my quiet hysteria. Gratitude and worry. I couldn't be certain what lay beneath her numbness or thinly covered her shock.

The hospital had given me the number of a county-supported crisis hotline. I talked to a trauma specialist twice. She recommended giving Liz space, a respectful distance, not drilling her with questions or forcing her to talk. "Talking," she said, "in and of itself does not resolve trauma." She recommended patience and the resumption of familiar routines. The trauma counselor said the person I knew and loved would be hidden for awhile.

Liz was not an intended target. She was an innocent, an accident. Wrong place, time. A victim of a random violent act. Acts. The reality of her broken body sat before us.

Profound, unsolvable human mysteries confront us. Who are we? Why are we here? Each of us explores these questions for ourselves. We cleave to religion. We embrace mother earth and peaceful loving kindness. We console ourselves with thoughts of the void. We become secular fiends, sports fanatics or repeat concert-goers, groupies who never get backstage. We say we've been here before or we say we cannot possibly know. Some of us are bothered by mystery and worry it like a mother thumbing rosary beads. Some don't think about it at all. And then there are mysteries we can't ignore, like how three teenagers can wreak such fierce savagery on their classmates and counselors and teachers. We carry that enigma in our minds, and Liz, carries it in her body for the rest of her life.

Instead of treading in sadness, swallowing more and more of it and bobbing at the sink line, my tendency with emotionally charged situations is to blow by the emotion and seek the rational. I surreptitiously read books about Columbine. I tried to reason out the unreasonable. Why would kids do this? How could any of them even consider it? Video games, TV, movies, novels, terrorism, endless war. Such saturation legitimizes violence, desensitizes all of us, provides models, but everyone is exposed and almost no one mimics. Social rejection explains nothing. Too pervasive, whereas mass-murder isn't. Mass school shootings tend to take place in small towns or rural areas and are committed by white boys. Columbine is the most glaring case. People think of it as the first of its kind. It wasn't. It had precedents. Liz keeps a list of them on her office wall. As for motives, look to psychology, stories of the shooters. Personality disorders take the rap. Psychopaths, psychotics, traumatized. But what, really, do labels explain? Personality disorders are akin to cancer. The origins are inexplicable, the outcomes often incurable.

Reading didn't help me understand. If anything, reading added to my frustration and sadness. Being instructed that people react differently to personal levels of violation was not new information. Our homeostasis always fluctuates with daily stressors—a bad cold, a change of residence, a new job, convoluted family dynamics, local and global politics. When shocks arrive in any of these, our equilibrium wobbles but eventually rights itself. Add in victimization and people become susceptible to more extreme reactions. Days and hours and weeks after a crime, victims pass through fatigue, sleeplessness, loss of appetite, numbness, denial, disbelief, anger, and eventually, hopefully, some form of recovery. Self-agency is key. I needed to watch for depressive signs, indications that Liz wasn't coping appropriately. *Appropriately.* Inappropriately would look like what? Because how the hell does one cope with such madness? Yes, the person I knew and loved would be hidden for a while.

As Liz sat on the deck, daydreaming, dozing, denying, wrapped tightly in blankets, trying to regain a sense of safety, I imagined the terror she must have felt internally, the terror rampaging through the school halls. And her, lying alone on the stairwell, her body crumpled in agony, frozen, scared to move or make noise, waiting, waiting to die, expecting to die. Was there room in that moment for anything other than terror? Had she died, my last words to her would have been, "See you when you get back. You'll have to get a cab, I'm working." And hers to me, quick, short, "Love ya, bye." Most people lead dull, quiet, uneventful lives. Liz and I were those people. We made our meaning. We created our fun. We took so much of our everyday lives for granted because we could, Liz because she'd matured without tragedy, and me, because I was blemished. I took our ease for granted because I found the idea of living any other way, in fear, in protest, whining about any of it, silly. I'd lost hard and I'd lost early. I'd survived. We are all genetic miracles, existing despite staggering odds. Every breath is a windfall regardless of the accompanying hardships. A couple years ago Liz and I took a trip to Arizona and walked the rim of the Grand Canyon and an hour or more along the Bright Angel trail. There are stretches of both that don't have rails or barriers where rough winds could knock a girl into the abyss.

My life in Seattle had mirrored my life in Cincinnati. At my managerial job at a restaurant, I ordered supplies, closed out previous days' transactions, and divvied time among crosswords and books and customer service. In Seattle, though, I was more social because of Liz and I owned a house and belonged to a gym because of Liz. When we first moved in, Liz maintained our lawn with an electric mower. I went to the art museum when she mowed in the rain. She'd bought me the membership. So long as the yard was tidy, and I got to arrange the interior of the house, I didn't mind what grew outside. In our first season, Liz eagerly put some flowers in the front yard and we were swarmed with bees. Then she tried a vegetable plot, but it drew slugs and dark, small bugs, so she returned the yard to its neat edges of grass.

After the incident—Liz refused to call it an accident, "there was nothing accidental about what those kids were doing"— when Liz was still learning to walk in her damaged body, we hired a Vietnamese couple to come monthly and take care of the yard. We had to fire them once Liz's hospital bills arrived and before we knew anything about a settlement. The backyard, once a square of perfect grass contained within a wooden fence, grew outlandish stalks of unnamed weeds and unruly patches of grass. When Liz started walking, I dug out a long patch of grass in the sunniest rectangle on the left. I leveled the ground and re-leveled the dirt. I filled the shape with white gravel and placed three large stones like ellipses, carefully spaced, hinting at what's missing or what's to come. I bought a bamboo rake so I could draw delicate ripples any time of day or night. My meditation practice, my site of spiritual repose. Gravel is purity, water is emptiness, distance. The larger stones are mountains, islands. The garden is a suspended landscape and point of inward departure. Many stone gardens include a water element like a koi pond or a cascading waterfall. Seattle provided plenty of moisture already. I didn't need an electric plastic rock waterfall intruding on my suspended, abstract world. I am not a religious person, religions being corrupt institutions portending the intentions of God. I leaned profane. Yet the garden did mollify me.

Liz walked. I raked.

About that time, I started getting headaches, so I went to see Liz's physical therapist. She kneaded the garbled tissue along the ridge of my skull and placed her hands lightly on my rib cage. She ever so gently shifted the rings and then tore into the tight muscles. The headaches disappeared. During those visits, I vented to her about Liz. I knew Liz was behaving in ways not consistent with recovery, but I couldn't say for certain what those ways were. Helpless in the face of her situation, and in turn, my situation, unable to imagine the cataclysm in her mind, I surrendered. I made allowances. There are people who use their pain, their broken bones, persistent headaches, their crumbling backs, to garner sympathy. Woe-is-me types. Liz was not wallowing, perhaps I was.

"Sounds like you might need to talk to someone," Tricia said, her hand cruelly probing my armpit.

"I did a round of therapy when I was younger. I just kept circling the same stories. I felt like I was going around a drain. I wonder what Dr. Clarissa Jenkins would think of me now." She was Ree's clinical psychologist. Ree gave Clarissa's daughter dance lessons so Clarissa would see me. "Do you think therapists wonder about their clients years later?"

"Of course they do. I know I do. I may not remember names, but I remember stories and conditions. There was an architect whose back wouldn't work when she rolled over in bed or the massage therapist whose knee clicks loudly during the quietest part of a session. The twenty-two-year-old with pelvic pain who couldn't have a gyn exam. We joked about her sending me a postcard about her cavernous vagina. That's what I love about this job. I get to hear all kinds of things about how people organize their lives. They tell me about their kids, their jobs, their childhoods, their politics, their cancers, their sex lives, their births and deaths. We work on their bodies all the while. Then they start to feel better. They're out of pain, they return to function, to their lives without physical therapy, and I'm left imagining the next installment. Working with people is my exercise in loss."

"What's the next installment for Liz and me?" I'd long been thinking that the marriage we had was not the marriage I wanted. "Don't answer that."

"Having some trouble?"

"It's not the War of the Roses," I said.

I turned onto my stomach, and Tricia worked the muscles on the back of my neck and along my spine. Her touch was skilled, not sensual, because her intention was clear, yet

I couldn't help drifting into fantasy. I knew about projection and transference. I drifted just the same. Happily married, a good listener, Tricia had strong knowing hands, a pleasant demeanor, and she knew her way around a pelvic bowl. As of late, she'd had her fingers inside my wife's pelvic bowl more than I had. A secondary effect of Liz's trauma and surgeries was vaginal and hip muscle dysfunction. A palpable difference in Liz's muscle tone denied me entry into her.

"I had a patient come through not too long ago. He'd come to be guardian of his niece after putting away his sister for drug trafficking. He was medically retired from the police force of some other city. He'd had a career of physical mishaps. Trauma and skirmish after violent skirmish. He'd been stabbed four times, shot once, thrown out of a third-story window. He'd been rolled over in his work vehicle. He was a MAN, but he was very soft spoken and gentle in here, and he had the softest hands. Crazy soft. Except for the scars and stories, you'd never guess what kind of trouble he'd seen. Anyway, the point is, people carry on. They get through. They get through a lot." I didn't deny it. People do come out on the other side of things. I just didn't know if I could cross over with Liz. She was forever marred. She would be forever baffled, wondering why her, why now.

"What happens when they don't get through? Certainly there are people who stall out."

"Liz isn't one of them," Tricia said.

I supposed not. I hoped not. Being thirteen years older, I assumed I would follow the natural course and die first, but there is no natural course, no predicting. Faced with a fresh void, I struggled to comprehend the emptiness of any amount of time without Liz. Yes, she was just across the room or out on the deck. I could see her, but I still spent many days without her. So, on Tricia's recommendation, I constructed the stone garden. Then, when Liz started her nighttime walks, distressed by the vacant house, I started staying late at the restaurant. I began having drinks with the staff, who were surprised and guarded at first, their soft, smooth faces giving nothing away. Eventually, Billy, one of the line cooks dared to ask, "Mind if we smoke? We usually smoke. It *is* legal now."

"Have at it."

He reached into a hidden jacket pocket and unearthed the fattest joint I'd seen in three decades.

"*That* can't be legal," I said.

Billy smiled and lit up. I watched as he, Jessica, Gavin, Mark, and Katie smoked themselves silly. They talked politics and art, briefly about how the night at work went. I envied their spry bodies and breezy conversation, their relative freedom. Gavin pulled his guitar from the storage room and strummed instrumentals. He unsubtly played to Jessica, and a twentysomethings seduction unfolded. I imagined their youthful, sleepless night, their exploration and acrobatics. All at once I ached for Liz. Fresh, thirty, bold, uncomplicated Liz.

After one of her adventures in gait and recovery, Liz sported a tattoo on the backside of her shoulder. And later, after I'd been to Ohio, bruises darkened the tops of her hands and wrapped around her wrists.

"Are you being safe?" I asked.

Ferries passed their daily commutes. Liz sat watching the endless motion.

"Liz?"

"Yes," she said. Then, as an afterthought, "As much as I can be."

"Liz, we're on the same side here."

She didn't respond, but I read her silence. We weren't on the same side because nothing had come along and wrecked my body. Just as she'd learned there are forces beyond her control, the same lesson was presented to me. I surrendered, but I was not pleased. "Liz, you know I'm here, right?"

She was a ghost wafting through our house.

"Don't disappear on me," I said.

We forgive what we can and surrender to the rest.

The problem was, I didn't know exactly what I was abiding. Liz was Liz, bodily, albeit damaged and inefficient. As for her mind and spirit, they were darkened as if a cloak had been thrown over them. But Liz was not drinking. She had not abandoned herself to religion. She was not pill-addicted, nor reading self-help books. She was not vegetating for hours in front of the television. She wasn't, as far as I could tell, having an affair. People had affairs for all kinds of reasons—the resurgence of that feeling of reckless abandon, romance, different attention, dizzying sexual obsession, boredom, lack of sex. I wasn't concerned about any of these in regard to Liz. The fact that she wasn't talking suggested that she wasn't moving through her grief or outrage, her victimization, the bad timing, the insanity. The fact that she wasn't talking meant she wasn't *processing*, or at least not in familiar, *appropriate* ways. But creating a coherent account of awful events, I was told, doesn't conclude it. Verbal and pharmacological treatment in the face of trauma are insufficient. But we were still having sex. Her physical therapy treatment had worked. I found my way to her again. Through our physical life, we were still communicating.

While Liz's rules might have changed, mine hadn't. I had allowed myself to enjoy a professional's hands touching me. I lingered over memories of an apprentice poet's skilled penmanship. Alexandra published two books. Incredibly, she'd accomplished what she said she would, "A book a decade, after thirty. The first two decades don't count." I knew how difficult it was to get published. David had denounced the industry for years. He had spreadsheets of rejections from journals and agents and presses. His first book was a literary memoir, recounting episodes of male nursing from his traveling days. Creative nonfiction always struck me as an oxymoron. David's second book blended forms and defied easy categorization. I made an appearance in it, as did Liz, against our wishes. When asked what his books are about, David says they're all about the same thing, how to *be* in the world, which is the working title of his third book. Once admitted, however, to the province of the published, David stopped denigrating the gatekeepers so vehemently. Alexandra never worried about getting published. She trusted, knew, that it would happen, and so it did. The power of forward thinking, perhaps. Manifest your destiny. Alex had been living and teaching in New Mexico for the past eight years. Tenured in her tanned skin and turquoise beads, her Birkenstocks and long fingers. Beyond rereading Alex's books and remembering her at twenty-five, all I learned about love and the body at that age, and beyond imagining Alex on the brink of sixty, the small act of raking stones soothed me. I hoped Liz would try it, staying within the majesty of our yard instead roaming on her unsafe wee-hour walkabouts. But she didn't. The stone garden remained my domain. Liz, my wife and family, stayed nearby. I was solitary as before.

When I was in college I threw away the few photographs I had of my family, those strangers. My history died with my brothers. Mothers carry the memories and stories. Mothers tell and reframe events, they remember different details. They help you understand your beginning and your present self, shaping who you are to become. Orphan that I was, I had no fixed history. I had no mother as reference and center. Yet more and more, as I raked the stones, I thought about my mother as I thought about how Liz was coping. My mother dropped out, completely wiping her mind with drugs. How does she see her life? The one before the train wreck, the one after, the one to come? Does she take stock? Does she think of me, of whom I've become?

Who *have* I become?

A stone-watcher. Witness to distant physicality—muscle, tendon, fascia, bone. Pain. Stumbling, awkward steps. Jangle of limbs. Walking as controlled falling. Witness to Liz. Her body, its incessant caterwaul. Witness to us. We are not grace. We are tragedy and recovery. Convalescence. I am standing by, helpless. Life in Cincinnati with its four distinct seasons, dating other people, David's judgments, tropical vacations, pain-free living, all of that, and everything else is behind us now.

CRANE

Most nights I go to bed alone but wake in the morning with Liz somewhere in the house. She has become owl-like, swooping through the neighborhood, feeding, exploring when no one sees, a harmless thief or spectator. She doesn't stay in the house at night. She roams. At first she traversed the few blocks of our neighborhood. Her range grew with her stamina, or with her anxiety or anger. Twice she called me from odd, far places to pick her up: downtown, in an alley of Pioneer Square; then on a beaten-down residential street in Columbia City. Neither were the safest locations at three in the morning. I have purchased several cans of pepper spray. I try not to worry. My melatonin dose has tripled in four months.

When Liz started walking at night, I started training wisteria along the back fence but not over it, not around to the adjacent fence, just along the side that faces the back of our house. I trimmed neatly, controlling the wisteria's suffocating spread. Then I added a fern garden. I wanted Jurassic-sized leaves, but because I didn't want to engage anyone at the nursery, I came home with seeds for some kind of fern. I planted them, and several weeks later, small, strong fiddleheads unrolled into fronds. They passed their adolescence under my haphazard care. The fence, wild with wisteria, backed a small corner rife with winding and unwinding ferns, contrasted the muted gray of the stone garden and the northwestern sky. My sanctuary. My still place and loose foundation.

Liz watched the ferries above the fence line and I watched the choking wisteria beneath it. Once, we snipped some ferns, sautéed and ate them. They were so bitter. I bought chimes and bird feeders and attracted hummingbirds with iridescent green feathers and shiny rose-choked throats. I'd always thought of myself as a city girl, but I became versed in the curious habits of black-capped chickadees. They hung upside down on branches to feed. They practiced monogamy and cavity, nesting together in vacant woodpecker holes. I learned to identify the irritating bark-scratch of the crazy red-eyed towhee. I knew not to look into its eyes. I abandoned museums. Nature supplied all—creation, distraction, destruction, salvation.

In February, I received a call from the Hamilton County Probate Office. Ree had died. As her next of kin, I needed to claim the body and tidy up her estate, which sounded too grandiose and official for the dilapidated brick one-bedroom house that couldn't host more than eight people comfortably for Thanksgiving dinner.

"Can David meet you there?" Liz asked when I asked her to accompany me to Ohio. "I can't deal with this right now."

"I don't want to go alone."

"Right, call David. I can't fly. Not yet."

"You weren't in a plane crash."

"It hasn't even been a year."

"What happens then? Everything gets better?"

Liz ignored my irritation. She said, "Just don't tell David anything. Even though he doesn't listen, he hears everything, and he'll put it in his next book, like how I look naked, making coffee."

I didn't correct her verb tense. She's no longer thirty and so free with her body. She looks different now, scarred-down and a little puffy. Her right leg holds more water than her left, a result of damage to lymph vessels in her leg and abdomen. Instead of discussing any of this, I tried to think of her on a segment of a hero's journey—in the refusal stage, the descent, which leads eventually to triumph. I just had to wait. Sometimes I even think of her as an addict who has to hit bottom before an ascent can begin, leaving her engaged and whole. Wishful thinking, perhaps, my struggle to hew redemption from the experience. Such effort was exhausting.

I flew to Chicago, where David agreed to pick me up. "I'm shocked that you called, Abigail," he said. We greeted one another with an overdue embrace, crammed my luggage into the secret storage of his Smart car and jammed ourselves into the bucket seats, knees kissing the dash. We had a five-hour drive ahead of us.

"I'm shocked you're bald, David." I touched his oily head affectionately. "You loved your hair."

"It's a solidarity thing. Charles' cancer and all. Mine as well, you could say. Much different though, melanoma." David unbuttoned his shirt to reveal pale, columbine scars dotting his chest. "Charles shaved his legs in support. Though I doubt he actually had to shave. That man has no hair as it is."

"Desert days?" I asked, nodding toward his chest.

"Desert days."

After one of his traveling contracts, David had stayed on in Sedona for several weeks, studying shamanism with a guru with two first names. David's study involved week-long vision quests, fasting in the sun and heat and darkness of the desert. While he had coated himself in spirit protection, he'd neglected to use sunscreen.

"Did you find what you were after?" I asked.

"Do we ever?"

Outside, snow dappled the air, dampening the roads but not slicking them. We were flanked by barren fields. I'd forgotten how flat and empty the Midwest feels with its tracks of endless land and sky.

"How is Charles? What's his prognosis?"

"That bastard refuses to see me," David said. After all these years he still hadn't learned to muffle his feelings with stoicism. "His beautiful ass has cancer and they implanted radiation beads in his prostate, but they aren't working. He agreed to the beads but he won't agree to surgery. Isn't it ironic? A man who came of age at Stonewall, survived the 80s, is going to let his glorious hole kill him."

"You are so crude, still so crude. He's married, David. He's always been married."

"She's his beard and knows it."

"Fifty years together binds people in ways we'll never understand. Anyway, he may change his mind. The heart has infinite capacity. You said that yourself years ago."

"Fuck you."

"Fuck me, then."

Talk of Charles made me remember that I had a father somewhere, leathered and thin, fishing in Florida, I supposed. With any luck he didn't drive a truck anymore. Maybe he owned his own boat or took tourists out on charters. Maybe he engaged with people differently, connecting in some small way, even if only over big fish. Maybe he was still agile and independent, a golfer or part-time stadium security guard.

I've reached the age when our parents begin their slow or fast processes of dying and friends acquire their own sad and strained diagnoses. IBS, MS, fibromyalgia, restless leg, autoimmune disorders with bizarre anthologies of symptoms, heart disease, diabetes, and, of course, cancer. When a friend was diagnosed with cervical cancer, she seemed to transform into it. Suddenly, we only talked about cancer and became hard-pressed to remember the type of friendship we had before the chemo and surgeries. What had we talked about before?

"You know, Abigail, I thought we'd moved away from one another for good and we'd have a deathbed phone call or two. We weren't so healthy together. I wasn't so healthy around you."

"No, you weren't, but I put up with you."

"You adored me."

"Most of the time."

"How is Elizabeth?" he asked, sincere for once. "Or is it Eliza? I guess I've never known."

"It's like time is currently suspended and we're having a small break in our marriage, living like roommates who share a bed. That's what I tell myself, knowing full well the untruth of that logic. I'm in a holding pattern. She's gone from the house a lot."

"With someone else?"

"I'm not finding stains on her clothes or love notes in her pockets. She's not dreamy and secretive or in love with someone else. She's doing something, though. She's elsewhere."

"Sexless roommates. That's sad," he said.

"We still have sex."

"How does *that* work?"

"The frequency isn't as high as it was in the past. Liz had some physical issues to get through. None of which would matter if she were talking to me. I read somewhere that marriage is a long patience. A succession of compromises."

"Life is a long patience," he said. "Everything settled from the Colorado thing?"

"As much as it can be. We still get the occasional call from journalists and psychologists."

"Vultures."

"Did you ever deal with shootings as a nurse?"

"Nothing in such quantity. Liz stumbled into the new guerrilla warfare, except it lacks ideology aside from chaos. You should give up trying to make any sense of it. Hold onto that patience, though. Liz is reconfiguring and reprioritizing. That's a normal response after a near-death experience. But don't let her write about it. Friends don't let friends publish bad prose. You should never have let me publish books one and two. Three is the winner."

"You *do* know you never show me anything you write until it's already in book form?"

"Whatever happened to all those girls you used to date? The arty ones?"

"Alex's second book, *Modes of Inauthenticity*, came out over the summer. She's teaching in New Mexico, last I knew, living the life she said she would. Tara's in Alaska. I get postcards from her every so often. She's painting now and lives without running water. She shits in an outhouse. Sucking the marrow, so they say."

"Oh, please, there's no marrow. What she's doing is a cliché, but that's not her fault. What almost everyone is doing is a cliché. And, really, most people don't even yearn to make something of themselves any longer. They're content to stare at their screens and finger the inane."

We drove in snowy silence for several miles approaching Whitestown and then Indianapolis, where we'd agreed to stop and stretch our legs. Indianapolis rivaled only DC for monuments dedicated to veterans. In Memorial Plaza, a hundred-foot phallus of black granite, bronzed at the bottom and gilded at the tip, was supposed to represent the nation's hopes. "Looks like a raised middle finger," David said as we craned our necks to take it in. Give me a sculpture garden any day, anything more original than a pillar jutting toward the sky. We made a few more loops around the fountain before getting back in the car. Soon, temperatures dropped with the sun and snow began to accumulate around us.

David pulled a stretchy black beanie from behind his seat. "For years Charles has used this ridiculous Sleep Shepherd hat," he said. "You can try to sleep if you want. I'm fine driving. Shep here has tiny speakers that give off pulses that are supposed to match brain wave frequencies. Shep matches yours, then slows itself so yours match his, slowing hypnotizing you to sleep. I stole it the last time I saw Charles. I just knew the fucker was going to cut me out."

I sat with the beanie in my lap. This is what Liz needs, I thought. Wrap her head in the black cloth and knock her out, keep her from wandering the streets at night, reset her brain waves, bring her back to herself. Sleep is crucial for happiness, intelligence, health, mood. We'd learned this first-hand when a smoke detector chirped at us at three in the morning. We couldn't find the detector in the kitchen or foyer, the laundry, or in any obvious place. It chirped at us every four minutes and forty-three seconds. Sleep deprivation is a form of torture, after all. Deprive me of sleep long enough and I'll relinquish any state or family secret. We found the detector stowed in a hidden storage compartment off the wall in the extra bedroom.

As I held the cloth in my lap, I imagined what Liz was doing in my absence. Probably tying her laces and setting out for a walk. We'd spent time apart when she traveled for work, but I'd never been the one to go away until now. When she and I first met, I saw couples who couldn't be apart as floridly insane. Then the need to be near Liz on a daily basis overtook me. I tried to resist my craving for her constant affection and attention, but I failed. She was the perfect woman for me.

The Chicago snow followed us into Cincinnati, all the way to Ree's house, which looked as I'd remembered. One wall had been completely converted into shelving. Ree lived perpetually in the 70s, holding tight to a Marantz stereo and crates of records, no iPod or CD player to be found. She did, however, allow production sound engineers to use any tools they wanted so long as whatever they did yielded to her vision. Her clothes, leotards, yoga pants, and flowy floral skirts and shredded jeans, all emanating the pervasive rusty, skunky mix of patchouli, incense, and marijuana, hung dustily in the closet, lay draped on her bed, or were left crumpled on the floor. She'd never been the tidiest of homemakers. A couple years into living with her, we often got mistaken for sisters, she being a young twenty-seven and me an old seventeen. Ree's clothes matched her personality, and while technically my size, they ill-fit my body. For years I traded among two pairs of jeans and several short-sleeve shirts, a function of budget and simplified deci-sion-making. I never once agonized over what to wear.

David left me at the door.

"Sure you want to drive in this?" I asked. Seattle rain had wiped my memory of snow, but looking past David at the ac-cumulating white, I remembered how slick the roads could be.

"This is nothing," he said. "I've driven through Vermont and North Dakota blizzards." He left, evidently co-piloted by his own memories. Since the age of sixteen, he'd refused and then lost and finally neglected contact with his parents. Right after I left to live with Ree, David emancipated himself, then lived in a friend's garage on and off for years between rounds in dorm rooms and strangers' beds. I had to admit he'd done well for himself.

In the house, a fine layer of dust covered Ree's books and the art on her walls, elegant advertisements for performances. As far as I could tell, in her later years she'd become a cat-lady without any cats. Beneath her bed lay a small, metal file-box. Inside, I found her birth certificate, social security card, some banking statements, her expired passport, and several death certificates. Beneath the documents, a false bottom opened onto several pills and a pipe and bag of marijuana. Without giving the idea much thought, I stuffed the pipe and smoked its small cavity's worth of weed. Ree's stash did not compare to Billy's jumbo joint. I sifted through the death certificates: Ree's parents, an aunt, an uncle, then my parents, my mother and father. All dead. Which seemed incomprehensible. Poof! Gone. As if they'd hardly been alive in the first place. The possibility of reconciliation or contact gone, too. My mother had died like her sons, in a car crash, though in Minnesota in the winter. Drunk? Sober? Car versus train? Car versus tree? Moose? The certificate didn't say. According to the paperwork, my father had died from cardiac arrest. I imagined a raging, seizing heart behind his ribs, uncontainable, unassuageable. I wondered whether he died alone and if his eighty-four years had satisfied him. He had never remarried. He and my mother had never divorced. Never bothered, I wondered, as in didn't care enough to, or did they hold some vestigial connection to one another that prevented either of them from filing papers? The second idea might be a means of consoling myself, though they were estranged longer than they were together, and they were absent from my life for decades. Ree alone had acknowledged and had closed out all these lives. She had spared me the obligation. I wondered if my parents had gravesites or were cremated and scattered. What places meant enough to them to be salted with their remains?

Ree had made her own arrangements, and had settled as much of her life as she could. She donated her body to medical research, which included transportation to the university from the coroner's office. When the students were done with her body, they were to cremate what was left and pass the cremains to me if I wanted them. Ree didn't care whether I spread the ashes in a special place or no place at all. She didn't care if I refused receipt. "I'll be dead," she'd written to me. "All the rites and rules about how to dispose of the dead are for the living. Do whatever feels right for you." Ree died from ALS. She had spared me this knowledge and had allowed Jersey to care for her. I felt an unhinged anger as I considered the injustice of a life-long dancer afflicted with a disease that took movement away. It happened all the time though. Agatha Christie with Alzheimer's. Mohammad Ali with Parkinson's. Thousands of runners with lung cancer. Children with anything. Benevolence doesn't govern the universe.

So many were gone and all at once. I reeled at my own fate. I was aging. I could feel it. I saw the signs. My period had become irregular, my moods unpredictable. Now toothpaste smudges in the sink or clothes left too long in the dryer, sent me into quick irritation. All my stabilities were under attack by time. Small circles of tan, dry spots appeared on my arms and hands. Hair grew where I'd never grown hair. Sag in my breasts. Sag in my arms. Sad girls. Sad arms. A state of bathos and self-pity, the aging body. Decreased endurance. Decreased drive. The mind mis-firing. Soon I'll be in my sixties, then seventies. Then? No more Abigail.

And Liz. The natural course and slow decline of her body, radically interrupted. Just before I'd left for Ohio, she'd moved out of a silent phase, playing the stereo for hours. Blasting heaves of bass. Joy Division. Joy. Division. I thought of a print I bought for her when we still lived in Cincinnati. Two panels of blue with a line in the middle. We discussed at length whether the line split or united the field. The artist said united, but did his intent really matter? We see what we want to see.

Sometime later, thumps on the front door and windowpane drew me outside where David had engaged neighbor kids in a snowball fight. His jeans were damp, and four shots landed on him for every one of his that hit a target. He was losing. I reached down and rounded snow between my hands and joined the fray. We volleyed for some time, ducking behind bushes and peeking around cars until the adults called their kids indoors. The streetlights had come on.

David and I flopped down onto the living room floor. We lay close, two sad siblings, orphaned years ago.

"Do you remember what Camus said?" I asked.

"'We must imagine Sisyphus happy.'"

"No, about love."

"'Mama died today, or maybe it was yesterday.'"

"Funny. He did have something special for mothers. But, no, I mean some quote about love being tragic and when it stops being tragic, then it's no longer love."

"We don't love what we have and love what we can't have and all that? That's not Camus," David said. "That's every thinker. The trick is to want what you have."

"Did what we have cease to be love a long time ago? And now it's tragic again because it's unrequited?"

"Now you're just being dramatic. What most people call love is really psychosis. Love is not tragic. It's a daily grind. The thing about marriage is that each person still exists in the world alone. And the fact is, the constancy of your love may not be what Liz wants right now. Charles doesn't want mine."

"I can't stop."

"Doesn't shut off, does it?"

"Life is a long patience," I echoed.

"Just hang onto something else Camus said, 'in the midst of winter, inside, there's an invincible summer.' He was a handsomely hopeful man."

After I said goodbye to David and returned to Seattle, I kept thinking of a trip Liz and I took to float the Deschutes River north of Bend, Oregon. We dragged nets of beer cans alongside our tubes. Liz, using Frisbees as paddles, moved us to shore, and on a sandy ledge we built a sandcastle with a moat and drawbridge from dry brush. I delighted in this quiet building together. I delighted in our stupid, playful grins. I am heartbroken and near tears, thinking of Liz flapping her arms and legs in the sand, making an angel. Doubtless, she has buried this memory while I recall the heat and sage and the dumb happiness in the sun.

I have to believe that time and mutual effort will bring us back together. Twenty years will turn our trials into a small hard season long past. The counselors recommend loving her and getting out the way. I still don't know what they mean. Where should I live in the meantime? The cells of the body renew every seven years. I just have to be patient. Liz will work the trauma out of her system as those cells die off one by one and new ones take their places. Fragile and dynamic, we can't hold on too tightly. We can't hold on at all because anything outside can be taken away. What's inside—that's what's reliable. I know Liz agrees, despite her loud guitars and too much treble. Nonetheless, I feel myself clutch at air, at words spoken before a judge to a woman who brought out the best in me, who brought me back to the world. A vow. Avow.

I pulled Liz's cello from the attic last week. Yesterday I saw notecards on the floor and desk in the office. On the cards:

CLAUSTROPHOBIC

CONTAGION

BREATHY

UNCERTAINTY

DARKNESS

DARKNESS

Some others. Beneath each one a music note. Did she tell you anything about them? When we first got together she told me about a performance she created in college. She called it an operetta. She'd had to generate a story and characters, then strip them away, leaving the elemental musical phrases and sounds. I hear the rough saw of the cello on occasion as I rake stones. I watch frenetic hummingbirds and listen to the see-to-lee of thrushes. I rake and drag, rake again. I look toward the house and listen. I clip and train wisteria. I battle the vine's strong arms. I rake and drag. In the morning, you'll see how the air and earth shift the stones in the night. But that's the point of the stone garden, isn't it? Constant change. Sorry euphemism for constant loss. I tend the fiddleheads. A few survived Liz's harvest. One day soon their gaunt fronds will strangle the sun.